BARBARA HELD

Mirror Image

First edition

ISBN: 978-1-7346417-0-7

Cover art by Katie Risor

This book was professionally typeset on Reedsy.
Find out more at reedsy.com

Dedication

I dedicate this book to my four grandchildren,
Laura, Anna, Emily and Ethan

I also dedicate this book, in loving memory, to my mom and dad,
Evelyn and Loren Watson.
Through family discussions, each of them provided additional details from
their younger years, some of which are included in this book.

Contents

Acknowledgement

I'd like to thank my loving husband, Greg, for his support in giving me the time and space needed to complete this project.

Also, thanks to my family and friends for their kind words, patience and encouragement over many years.

A special thanks to friends who have helped edit and especially my writers' group, Yarnspinners, who were always so kind and patient.

I

Part One

1

The Fight

J ennifer, dressed in blue jean shorts, a red tank top and sneakers headed outside to work in her flower garden. Her short, brown, curly hair held barrettes at each temple to hold her hair out of her blue eyes.

"Don't even think about it, Jennifer," said Mom. "I've told you for a week you have to clean your room and it still isn't done. You also have dishes to do. Your flowers will have to wait until your chores are done."

"But Mom, I cleaned my room. I brought all the dirty dishes down and threw out the old food," said Jennifer.

"That was barely a start. You have to *clean*. Pick up, put away, dust and vacuum. I let you go to the movies last night because you *promised* me you would clean first thing this morning and it still isn't done. This time, I will not give in."

Jennifer sighed. She might as well go clean her room.

Her parents had given her a spot along the house to plant flowers. She'd planted bright yellow daffodils and red tulips for early blooming. The lilac, pink and white petunias were blooming now and needed weeding. This being her second year, she had already learned petunias bloomed all summer and spread so they filled every empty space.

As Jennifer started picking up dirty clothes, she thought again how much she loved working with flowers. She had asked for a little spot for vegetables but both parents had said no to that suggestion. They had grown up on farms and wanted nothing further to do with "all that work." *How could anyone think growing things was a lot of work?* Jennifer loved working in the dirt, planting the seeds and bulbs and watching the flowers grow. She knew she would feel the same about vegetables and they would be healthy to eat. Mom was all about eating healthy.

Jennifer picked up two pairs of blue jeans, white jean shorts, two t-shirts, one lilac and one green. Reaching under the bed, she pulled out another pile. *There's my blue halter top.* She'd been looking for that when it was so hot last week. She also found her swimsuit and towel, still damp from swimming earlier in the week. She hauled an armload of dirty clothes to the laundry and returned to her room.

While putting away a stack of clean clothes, the phone rang. Jennifer reached for the phone on her desk, not a cell phone like all her friends had but at least she had an extension in her room.

"Hey," Jennifer said to her best friend, Paige.

"Jen, I've got some awesome news."

"Oh my gosh!" squealed Jennifer, jumping up and down, after hearing the news. "You actually got tickets to Take Five? I thought they were sold out."

"My mom got them for us. You, me and Kelly. We need to know like right now if you can go."

"I'm sure Mom will let me. I mean, it's *Take Five*! I'll call you right back."

Jennifer went to find Mom, not nearly as confident as she'd been on the phone.

She had promised Mom she would clean her room first thing this morning, but she had slept in, then called several friends and hadn't gotten around to cleaning her room.

And the dishes. What's with that anyway? Everyone had a dishwasher, except them. They certainly could afford one with Mom being a dietitian and Dad a lawyer. She wouldn't complain if she just had to fill and empty a dishwasher. She had more important things to do than to stand and wash dishes, then dry them and put them away. That was just nuts.

Jennifer may have neglected some of her chores, but she'd been taking good care of her little brother, Ryan. Before summer break, her mom had made her take a babysitting course through the American Red Cross. Now, Jennifer took care of Ryan while her parents were at work. As little brothers go, he was pretty OK for a seven-year-old. He often entertained himself with his trucks, hauling endless piles of sand around.

Her dad made a sand box years ago and Ryan would spend hours playing by himself. When he wasn't in the sand box, they played games—Go Fish or Crazy Eights—or she read to him or helped with puzzles. Her parents told her she was pretty responsible for an eleven-year-old and had a good head on her shoulders. Keeping Ryan safe was something she took seriously. That should count for something. With that thought in mind, Jennifer went looking for Mom.

She was in the kitchen baking. A taller version of Jennifer, except her hair was blond, shoulder length, pulled into a pony tail. The same dimples in her cheeks made her look younger than her thirty-eight years. Flour covered her jeans and shirt from the Johnny cake she just put in the oven. A perfectionist when it came to keeping her house clean and a pretty good cook, but truly messy in the kitchen.

"Mom, I have a really big favor to ask you," said Jennifer .

"I'm not in a mood to grant you favors right now. Your room isn't clean and the dishes are still in the sink."

"I know Mom, and I'm sorry, but this is really, really important. Paige's mom got tickets to Take Five. They were supposed to be sold out but she got them for Paige and Kelly and me and the concert is tonight and I have to let her know like right now." Before her mom could answer, Jennifer rushed on. "I *really, really, really* promise to clean my room spotless tomorrow and keep the dishes done. Please, Mom, please."

Jennifer finally took a breath and waited for the response. Her mom looked at her firmly and stated what Jennifer saw in her mom's eyes. "I'm sorry, Jennifer. I don't think so. I've been asking you for a week to clean your room. You promised me you would do it this morning when I let you go to the movies last night and it *still* isn't done. You've been neglecting your chores."

"But Mom, this is really important! This is *Take Five*. They're always sold out. It's a miracle we even got tickets."

"I'm sorry, Jennifer. My decision stands."

"That's not fair! This is a really big deal! You know I love Take Five and it probably will be the only chance I ever get to see them. You're just being mean."

"That's enough, young lady. The answer is no."

Jennifer glared at her mom in disbelief and then stomped out of the kitchen. Running up to her bedroom, she barely managed not to slam the door. Throwing herself on her bed, she dissolved into tears. Wracking sobs shook her whole body. Mom knew how much she loved this group. You could hardly see the lilac colored walls of her room because of the posters she had of Take Five. She had every CD they made. Mom and Dad even approved of them. They weren't the kind of group that just made obnoxious noise, as Mom called it.

Jennifer hadn't called Paige back, but knew she had to. Mom wasn't going to change her mind. She might as well get the inevitable over with and let Paige know she couldn't go.

Still stalling, Jennifer went into the bathroom to wash her face. She knew her eyes were puffy and red and her face blotchy from crying. As she finished, she looked in the mirror and stared. Something was wrong. The image in the mirror was different. She saw the same curly brown hair, the same deep blue eyes, but they were not red and puffy. The same round face with dimples in each cheek but not blotchy from crying. And the girl in the mirror was smiling. Jennifer knew she wasn't smiling. Startled, scowling, perplexed, confused, mystified maybe. But certainly not smiling.

Could the girl see Jennifer? She didn't think so. She certainly didn't look perplexed. The girl was laughing now. It was like a video of someone in the bathroom mirror who looked just like her. Almost. It didn't make sense.

Jennifer slowly lifted her hand and touched the mirror. As soon as she did . . .

2

The Fall

Jennifer's fingers sank into the mirror. She felt herself being pulled with intense force.

"No! Please, no!" She felt her fingers, then her hand, then her arm being drawn in. She strained with all her might to release her arm but couldn't pry it lose. Her eyes wide with fear, she kept trying to wrench her arm free but the force was too strong.

A scream tore out of her, as her whole body was pulled into the mirror. She could see nothing. Not even her own body. No color. No light. Everything was pitch black. She felt herself whirling around and around. Feeling dizzy, she closed her eyes tight. She screamed again but no one was there to hear. Her heart pounded in her chest. She had never been so afraid. And then, she was falling and could do nothing to stop it.

She landed suddenly, hitting something hard. Jennifer lay there for what seemed like a long time, the wind knocked out of her. She kept her eyes closed, trying to gauge what had happened. How could she have fallen into her bathroom mirror? She felt dazed and scared.

Her breathing slowed. Her body hurt all over.

"Aunt Harriet, Julie's fallen out of the tree again," someone yelled Jennifer heard running and someone asking if Julie was all right. A dog barked in the distance. She heard the commotion around her but could not, would not, open her eyes.

"Julie? Julie? Can you hear me?" asked someone close. Jennifer didn't know if Julie could hear, but *she* sure could. *Who is Julie?* Someone was talking right in her ear. "Oh please, Lord," said the voice, "please may Julie be all right."

"Jack, run and get Uncle Norman," said the voice.

Jennifer slowly opened her eyes. She looked directly at a woman with dark hair pulled back into a bun and a very worried expression in her green-eyed oval face. She was wearing a dress with tiny blue and white flowers over which was a full yellow apron.

"Are you all right, Julie?" said the woman looking right at her and rubbing Jennifer's arms and legs. "Can you answer me? Does anything feel broken? You really have to stop climbing that tree. It's too high. And far too dangerous."

Jennifer tried to sit up but couldn't. Her back and head hurt. She ached all over like she had ... well, fallen out of a very tall tree. But Jennifer knew that wasn't the case. She knew moments ago she had been standing in her bathroom at home.

"Where am I? Who are you?" asked Jennifer. The woman's worried expression returned, her brow furrowed and her mouth grim.

"It's Mom, Julie," replied the woman. The woman must have seen the panic in Jennifer's eyes, because she hurried on. "Just stay calm. You'll be all right. You just had a bad fall."

"My name is not Julie! I'm Jennifer. You are not my mother!" shouted Jennifer, her panic rising again. "Please get my mother. I need my mother!" Jennifer breathed faster and faster but still couldn't get enough air. Her eyes grew big, her gaze darting back and forth as her panic grew.

"Please," begged Jennifer, "please get my mother. She'll know what to do."

A golden and brown collie came out of nowhere and ran up to her. He sniffed tentatively and then backed away. He came to her again and sniffed, this time licking her arm.

"Move away, Pal," said the woman. "You can't help right now. Honey, please try to relax. It doesn't appear you have any broken bones so we'll carry you into the house. Here comes your dad now."

Relief flowed through Jennifer. Dad was coming. He was strong and smart. He would fix everything.

The man running toward her was tall and thin wearing a blue short-sleeve shirt, overalls and work boots. He had a long thin face, long nose, blue eyes, big ears and unruly brown hair. Deep concern in his eyes as he bent down beside her, he gently took her small hand in his large hand. But he was not Dad.

"How are you doing, Princess? Did the tree get you again?"

"You're not my dad! I'm not Julie and I'm not a princess! My name is Jennifer and I want to go home. I did *not* fall out of a tree. I fell into a mirror. Please take me home."

Jennifer couldn't take it anymore. She started to cry, at first small whimpers that turned into heaving sobs. Hadn't she just been crying this hard over something else? She gulped air trying to get her breath.

"Please calm down, dear," said the woman. "Norman, carry her into the house. I'll call Dr. Baxter."

As Norman picked her up, Jennifer's sobs continued.

3

The Facts

Jennifer once again looked into the concerned eyes of someone she did not know. He looked really old, maybe fifty, with hair so blond it looked almost white. He had a beard and wire-rimmed glasses perched on the end of his nose, a stethoscope around his neck, and a black bag sat beside him. Observing her carefully as he checked her arms and legs, Jennifer knew he must be Dr. Baxter.

After further examination, he said, "It appears you're right, Harriet. I don't feel any breaks this time. Do you know who I am?" he asked, looking at Jennifer.

"Dr. Baxter?" Jennifer guessed.

"That's right. Good girl. And do you know your name?"

"Jennifer Marie Freeman."

"OK, honey, you rest," he said while patting her arm. "I'm going to talk to your folks."

Jennifer closed her eyes, barely containing the scream of frustration on her lips. When she opened her eyes the three adults were gone but she could hear them talking in the next room.

Dr. Baxter was saying, "I'm sure it's a temporary memory loss. She doesn't appear to have any other symptoms of the fall. Keep a close eye on her the next few days. If her memory doesn't come back, I'll put her in the hospital for further tests."

Harriet said, "Today is Saturday. Let's let her rest, no chores anymore this week end. Maybe we could go fishing after church tomorrow if she's up to it. She really likes fishing and it would be relaxing. Maybe that would stir her memory."

Norman said, "That sounds good. I hope her memory returns soon. It really hurts to have her look at us and not know who we are."

Listening to them, Jennifer felt sad. She didn't mean to hurt them but she was *not* Julie. Maybe she could at least try to be nice until things got sorted out.

Jennifer looked around. She found herself in a small, pink bedroom with one window and frilly, white, lace curtains. The full bed had a white bedspread with little knobs all over it. She also noticed a large bureau and a little desk with attached mirror, both painted white. A framed picture of wild flowers hung on the wall along with two small paint-by-number pictures of horses like the ones her grandma painted. A bookcase filled with books sat in a corner. *Wow. Mom would love this Julie person. Not one thing's out of place. It looks kind of nice.*

Jennifer could smell wonderful aromas coming from somewhere. She couldn't place all the scents, but picked out the sweet cinnamon smell of apple pie, her favorite.

Harriet poked her head in the doorway, "Do you think you could eat something? Supper is about ready."

"Yes. I'm starved. It smells wonderful. I just have to clean up first. Can you, um, tell me where the bathroom is?"

"The bathroom? You mean the sink?"

"Well, yes, and to go to the bathroom." Jennifer felt her face become hot, embarrassed to have to ask for something so personal from this stranger.

"Well, the sink is in the kitchen by the pump and of course the outhouse is outside."

"No, no. This is really weird, but I mean the *bathroom*. Sink, tub, shower, toilet. All in one. You know. Bathroom."

"Honey, I know there are people who have all that. But not us. Come, I'll show you. You'll remember."

Jennifer followed her out of the bedroom with growing apprehension. They walked through a small room with cupboards and counters. Curious, Jennifer decided to ask about that later. They continued into the kitchen, through an enclosed porch and outside. When Harriet pointed to a little pink building at the far end of the yard, Jennifer cringed. She had heard of outhouses from her grandparents, but never had to use one.

Nobody in this day and age should have to use an outhouse.

"Do you need help?"

Jennifer thought she would die. Her face felt even hotter and she barely managed to say, "No, I can do it."

Slowly she started toward the outhouse. She had no choice; she needed to go to the bathroom and this was it. She had heard horror stories about spiders, bugs, and mice living in outhouses.

As she reached the door, she took a deep breath and opened it. What a surprise! The outhouse was totally pink, inside and out. A small window high up gave some light and not a spider or bug in sight. It was spotless. Actual toilet paper hung for use and not the catalog pages she had also heard about. A two-seater. Why, Jennifer couldn't imagine. *Would people actually go to the bathroom on a buddy system?*

Jennifer finished quickly and left, feeling that she had overcome a hurdle.

Harriet led her back inside, directing her to the sink in the corner of the kitchen. A round, white metal dish with red trim, about twenty inches in diameter sat in a space cut in the top of the counter. Beside the sink was a red hand pump and soap, with a washcloth and towel hanging on a towel bar. Jennifer had seen pumps in parks and knew she had to move the handle up and down to get water. She was nonetheless excited when water actually flowed out into the white dish. She washed quickly in the cold water and headed to the table for supper.

On the way to the table, Jennifer noticed a calendar from the De Soto State Bank hanging on the wall. "Why do you have such an old calendar?" she asked.

"Did I forget to flip the page again?" said Harriet. "It seems I always get too busy and forget." As she stepped over to look, she added, "Oh, no. This is right. July 1958."

Jennifer felt her panic rising again. This was too much. Nineteen fifty-eight was what, about forty years before she had been born! She turned her back to Harriet and Norman, and put her head against the wall, willing herself to stay calm. If she lost it again, she might be taken to a hospital. What kinds of hospitals did they have in 1958? How could she have been transported back in time through her bathroom mirror? How could she get home again? And how would she stay out of the hospital until that happened? She couldn't imagine how horrific the hospitals had been that long ago. She had seen old war movies and the conditions were terrible.

"Are you all right, honey?" asked Norman. "You're white as a ghost."

"Yes," replied Jennifer. "Just dizzy. And I have a headache. I'll be all right."

Slowly Jennifer walked over to the table and sat down to eat trying to figure out what to do next.

4

The Farm

Still dazed, Jennifer sat through supper, not enjoying the pork chops, mashed potatoes, gravy, peas, homemade buns, nor even the apple pie she had smelled earlier.

"I thought you were hungry," said Harriet. "You've hardly eaten anything."

"I know. I'm sorry. It's really good. I just can't eat. I'm trying to remember what hap … stuff. If you don't mind, maybe I'll walk around the house and try to remember."

Curious, Jennifer wondered what else might be *way* different than what she was used to.

It sure explained the pump and outhouse.

"Of course, we don't mind," said Norman. "This is your home."

Jennifer started at the room she had seen earlier, with the cupboards.

"That, of course, is the pantry," said Harriet. "We've washed a lot of dishes and made a lot of pies and cookies in there."

Not very big, maybe five feet by seven feet. Cupboards and counters covered two walls and against another wall a table that held two large, round, silver pans flipped over. She peeked in one cupboard and saw dishes: plates, cups, glasses, and bowls. In another, foodstuffs: cereal,

15

coffee, flour, sugar. In a drawer she found silverware and utensils. Even though they said this was her home, she knew it wasn't, and it felt like invading their privacy.

She continued on through the bedroom she had been in earlier and into another bedroom that must be Harriet and Norman's. There was a full bed, chest, and dresser with a big mirror in the middle, and drawers low on each side. A short stool sat in front of the mirror. The curtains were lightweight, see-through white with little, white fluffy flowers throughout. The room was painted a light green. Except for a picture of Jesus on one wall, the walls were bare.

Jennifer continued around and came into the living room. She saw a brown couch and matching chair, desk, old TV, and a stereo for playing old-fashioned records. It looked a lot like the one her grandma had. A big black phone sat on a little table next to the chair. Brown, flecked carpet covered the floor, the only room with carpeting. She noticed a picture of two girls smiling. One of them could have been her sister. *This must be the "missing" Julie.*

She hadn't thought about it before, but if she was here instead of Julie, where *was* Julie?

In her investigation, Jennifer saw only one TV, one radio, one phone, and no computers. *These people really did live in the Dark Ages.*

The tour made a full circle. By the time she got back to the kitchen, Harriet was doing dishes. She had flipped the two big pans Jennifer saw earlier, washing in one, rinsing in another, and piling the dishes to drain on a dish towel.

"Can I dry?" Jennifer asked before she thought about what she was saying. *I can't believe I just asked that. Mom had to ask me repeatedly to do dishes.*

"If you feel up to it, that would be nice," said Harriet. "How are you feeling?"

"I have a little headache and my body aches but otherwise I'm OK."

Jennifer remembered where she had seen the plates, glasses, and silverware and put those away as she dried.

Harriet started humming a song as she washed dishes.

"What is that song?" asked Jennifer. "It sounds familiar."

"It's *Amazing Grace*. We sing it in church a lot." Harriet started singing and Jennifer joined in where she knew the words.

When they had finished the song, Jennifer said, "Tell me about stuff. Just general stuff. Things that might help me."

"Well, your dad is a farmer and has been all his life. He ..."

"What kind of farmer? Does he grow things or raise animals?"

"Both. We have cows and pigs. We grow hay and oats, wheat, tobacco."

"You grow tobacco?" Jennifer asked.

"It's a cash crop to help pay for necessities. Why do you ask?"

"Couldn't you grow something different for cash? Something that doesn't make people sick?"

"Everyone around here grows tobacco. Why do you think it makes people sick?"

"It causes cancer." Seeing Harriet's expression, Jennifer added, "I must have heard that somewhere, that it's bad for people and causes cancer."

"Well, I've never heard that. You should talk with your dad about that."

When done with dishes, Jennifer said, "It was fun singing and talking. It makes time go faster. I think I'll go outside now and look around. I'm still hoping something will come to me." *Liar.*

"Do you want me to come along?"

"If you want to."

Walking out the door, they saw Jack, his red shirt flying as he played with Pal. Jack wore jeans and white tennis shoes needing a good washing. His brown hair was cut close to his head and his brown eyes sparkled with mischief.

"Jack, do you want to go for a walk with Julie and me?" asked Harriet.

"Sure," said Jack, running ahead of them.

Pal followed, running and jumping in circles around Jack, waiting for him to throw the stick he held in his hand.

"He's very pretty," said Jennifer. "I always wanted a dog."

"Well, that's good," replied Harriet, "because we've had him now for five years and you two are almost inseparable."

"Hi, Pal," said Jennifer, putting her hand out to the dog.

Sniffing, Pal slowly approached her.

"That's odd," said Harriet. "He acts as if he doesn't know you. Maybe because you don't remember him, he feels something different."

"Yeah, that's probably it." Jennifer stooped to pet him, Pal sniffing her the whole time.

Jennifer noticed a pretty little flower garden full of pansies and petunias. Lilac, yellow, white, pink, and red covered the space and a wonderful sweet smell filled the air.

"Ooh, how pretty," said Jennifer. "I just love flowers."

"I know you do. You did this all by yourself."

An outside pump, gray with a tall windmill towering over it stood about thirty feet from the back door. A small, brown building stood behind.

"What is that building?" asked Jennifer.

"That's the milk house. That's where we bring the milk to get ready to be picked up by the milk truck."

"Bring it from where?"

"From the barn, after milking the cows." Harriet motioned toward the big, red barn across the driveway. Jennifer could see a few black and white cows, some grazing and others drinking from a water trough.

"Why are you telling Julie about the milk house and cows?" asked Jack. "She lives here, you know."

"Well, Jack, because of her fall earlier, Julie is having a hard time remembering things. I'm trying to help her."

"Really? You mean you can't remember anything? That would be so neat. Do you know who I am? I'm your cousin. Our dads are brothers. I come here sometimes when my mom and dad want to do something without me, like shop. That's OK with me. I would rather come here and play with Pal. *He sounds like Ryan. He doesn't like to shop either, unless it's for trucks.* Do you remember the time Aunt Harriet had to run from the outhouse to the windmill to get away from the bull?"

"Why no, I don't. I don't remember anything."

"That was so neat. The bull got out and Aunt Harriet ran to the outhouse because it was closer, but then the bull was butting the outhouse and she thought maybe it would push it right over, so she made a run for it and climbed the windmill. I would say she sure is a fast runner!" Jack, almost breathless in his excitement, continued. "She had to stay up on the windmill until Uncle Norman came home to take the bull away."

Fearful, Jennifer turned a circle looking in every direction.

"Don't worry. They got rid of that bull pretty quick after that."

Jennifer, Harriet, Jack, and Pal continued their walk. Gray siding covered the house. Tiger lilies adorned one side of the house, giving off a strong sweet scent, and peony bushes, full of big, pink blossoms, brightened up the yard. A board swing swayed from a large branch of a huge oak tree in the front yard. A tall tree, Jennifer wondered if it was the tree she supposedly fell out of. A large tractor tire laid flat and painted white, filled with more petunias, sat next to the mailbox. Harriet or Julie must love flowers as much as she did.

On the other side of the house she saw clotheslines and beyond, a huge garden.

"Oh, you grow your own vegetables?" asked Jennifer.

"We sure do. You help a lot with weeding, picking, and canning. I don't know what I'd do without your help."

"Can I go look?" asked Jennifer.

"I don't think we should. That's enough exercise for you today. We'll see how you feel tomorrow."

As the two of them walked back into the house, Jennifer felt her plight could have been worse. She had popped into a place with good people, lots of flower gardens, a vegetable garden, *and* a dog. Until she figured out how to get home, maybe this wasn't such a bad place to have fallen into.

5

The Fright

As Jennifer and Harriet walked back into the house, Harriet said, "I'll fix you a foot basin so you can wash up a little before some television."

"Awesome."

The foot basin looked like the wash basin only bigger, reminding her of the turkey roaster her mom used at Thanksgiving. When ready, Jennifer took it to Julie's room, along with a wash cloth and towel. She quickly washed as well as she could without a bathtub or shower, put on pajamas, and headed for the living room.

Norman and Harriet were just settling in to watch TV. Worn out from the day's stress, it would feel good to sit and relax.

"What are you watching?" asked Jennifer.

"Our normal. *The Lawrence Welk Show*," said Norman.

You've got to be kidding. Women in long, ugly dresses and men in tuxedos singing "Danny Boy" and "Some Enchanted Evening" was not her idea of fun. Then people would go waltzing across the stage with bubbles floating all around. What kind of a program was this? *Kelly and Paige get Take Five and I get this.*

"Maybe there's a movie on or something ... else," suggested Jennifer.

"A movie? Something else? We only have the one channel," said Harriet. "This is a great program. I just love the songs and watching the dancers glide across the floor. You never minded before."

Rolling her eyes so they couldn't see, her gaze landed on the picture of Julie and her friend. She went over and picked up the picture to study it.

"That's you, of course," said Norman, "and your best friend, Grace. She'll be in church tomorrow."

"We're going to church?"

"We always do, dear," said Harriet. "Maybe you'll wake up tomorrow and remember everything. If not, Grace might help. You've been best friends since first grade."

"She's pretty," Jennifer said. Grace had long, straight, blond hair and bright blue eyes. She and Julie were both laughing. *I wonder what they're laughing about. Paige and Kelly and I could laugh over nothing, just sitting around.*

"Yes, she is, but so are you," replied Norman. "You two are like peas in a pod."

The next few minutes of the show consisted of an accordion player with a ridiculous smile. *I can't take any more of this.*

"If you don't mind, I think I'll go to bed. It's been a weird day." *Talk about an understatement!*

"OK, good night," said Harriet and Norman in unison.

"Sleep tight, Princess," said Norman, wincing as soon as he said it, no doubt remembering the last time he called her princess.

Jennifer escaped to Julie's room. She felt some relief being away from Harriet and Norman. As nice as they were, she felt their gaze on her all the time. Watching for some sign of remembrance, a look of recognition, an *aha* moment. She also knew that moment would never come and she didn't know what to do.

When she didn't remember, couldn't remember, what if they took her to the doctor for more tests? What if the doctor put her in the hospital, and kept her for good?

Maybe Grace could help her. Could she tell Grace the truth? Would she believe her? If she did believe her, Grace could tell Jennifer all about Julie. Or would Grace tell someone else who, thinking Jennifer was crazy, take her to the hospital anyway?

Looking for something to wear to church the next day, she noted there wasn't a lot to choose from. *I had more clothes under my bed when I was cleaning than Julie has in her whole closet.* She found a navy dress with cap sleeves and a big, white collar, with red and white stripes on the front. Nope. Too nerdy. Deciding on a pair of jeans and pink T-shirt with a scallop along the neck, she laid them out for the next morning and crawled into bed.

With everything on her mind, sleep evaded her. Tossing and turning, she threw her covers off and still felt too warm.

It must be ninety degrees! Why is it so warm? She realized she hadn't seen any type of air conditioner. *How can they stand this heat without an air conditioner, especially at night when trying to sleep?*

As she lay there, she thought about Kelly and Paige. They would be at the concert now, having a wonderful time. Did they miss her? Maybe, but they would have a good time anyway. That was OK. Even if she was home, she knew she wouldn't be at the concert. Mom had made that abundantly clear. She wished she could tell her mom right now she was sorry. The concert somehow didn't seem as important as it had a few hours earlier.

Mom and Dad will be watching some old movie on TV. Ryan might be in bed already. What time is it back home? Is Julie there instead of me? Or are Mom and Dad going bonkers thinking I've snuck out of the house to go to the concert anyway?

She tossed and turned for a long time, worried about everything, including what to do with Grace. *Should I tell her the truth and hope she believes me and keeps her mouth shut? Or should I pretend I'm Julie and maybe Grace won't notice any difference? I'd better wait and see what happens.* When she finally fell asleep, her dreams were filled with mirrors and different images of herself floating in space.

She woke in the night and had to go to the bathroom. She did not want to go to the outhouse at night. What if there were wild animals? She lay there for a long time, not able to go back to sleep. Finally, she decided she had to make the trip outside. Maybe she could see well enough to go quickly.

Quietly getting out of bed, she headed for the door. Moving slowly and carefully by touch, she finally managed to make it to the back door without waking Norman and Harriet. When she opened the outside door, a wonderful cool breeze washed over her. She stood for a moment taking in her surroundings. A full moon and stars lit up the night sky, the air fresh, no smog, no glow in the sky from cities in the distance, no traffic noises. No horns. No sirens. *How calm and peaceful.*

Looking across the yard, the outhouse seemed farther away than she remembered. She watched for any wild animals that might be lurking and started across the lawn. After all, this was in the middle of wild country, no towns around for miles. Out of the corner of her eye, she saw movement. She turned to protect herself until she saw Pal racing toward her. As he approached, he slowed and started sniffing.

"Hi, Pal. I know you know I'm not Julie but I still want to be your friend." She reached out. He slowly came up to her and sniffed. She scratched behind his ears and petted his head.

"OK, boy. You stay here and guard while I go do my thing, OK?" Jennifer hurried in and when she came out, Pal was sitting right where she'd left him.

"You're a good boy. Thanks, Pal." Jennifer headed back to the house feeling relieved. Suddenly, something swooped down, almost hitting her head. Something small. Moving fast. Jennifer couldn't tell what it was. She stopped in her tracks but could see nothing. She took two steps. Again, she felt something swoop close to her head. Screaming, she ran toward the house, covering her head with her arms. As she reached the back door, Norman and Harriet were coming out.

"What's wrong? What happened?" asked Norman.

"Something came after me! I had to go to the bathroom and when I came out, something kept attacking me. I don't know what it was. I couldn't see."

Norman looked around but saw nothing dangerous. They took Jennifer into the house and tried to calm her.

"What did it look like? Was it big, maybe like a pig that got out?"

"No. It was little and fast. I couldn't see but it swooped by my head. I thought it was going to bite me."

"Oh," said Norman. "I bet it was a bat. They fly at night and eat lots of insects. I don't think it would have hurt you."

Jennifer calmed down as they tucked her back into bed.

As Harriet left the room, she said, "If you have to go to the bathroom again, use the chamber pot." *The what?*

Jennifer, exhausted from the day's events still couldn't sleep. She thought about her home. She missed her shower where she could get really clean and wash her hair. She could soap up and take a long time to rinse and enjoy the warm water splashing over her. *Who would think I would miss a bathroom? It's a pain to have to go outside. What if it was raining or winter? What did Harriet say? Use the chamber pot? What in the world is a chamber pot? I just bet it's not as convenient as the bathroom I have at home.*

She woke with sun streaming in her window and a gentle breeze blowing tree branches outside. It took Jennifer a minute to remember what happened.

Well, I guess it's not a dream.

She heard movement in the kitchen and crawled out of bed. Donning the jeans and top she laid out the night before, she went to start her day.

"Morning," she said, while entering the kitchen.

"Good morning," said Harriet and Norman, again in unison, both with questioning looks in their eyes.

"Why didn't you dress for church?" asked Harriet. "We'll be leaving shortly after breakfast."

"I am ready. This is clean and looks nice."

"No, we don't wear jeans to church. You must remember that much. You can change after you eat. You have that cute navy dress or your skirt and blouse."

Jennifer didn't know what to say. Lots of people wore jeans to church. To be honest, she would rather wear a dress or skirt, but not the nerdy ones she had found in Julie's closet.

"Sit down and eat. Then you can change," Norman confirmed.

Jennifer sat. Norman said grace and they all said amen.

"Would you like Cheerios or Corn Flakes?" asked Harriet.

Jennifer had noticed a big bowl of strawberries on the table. "I would like strawberries. Can I have them?"

"You always get hives from the strawberries," said Harriet.

"I think I'll give it a try," said Jennifer, hoping she wouldn't get hives. They never bothered her before.

Harriet passed Jennifer the bowl of big, red strawberries and she spooned some into her bowl, adding a little sugar and milk. She popped one in her mouth and closed her eyes, savoring the sweet, juicy taste. Spreading a slice of fresh homemade bread with butter, she took a bite. Warm homemade bread! *When was the last time I had warm homemade bread with butter and fresh strawberries? Never!* Each strawberry was just as sweet and juicy as the last and the bread soft and delicious. She noticed Norman dunking his bread in his coffee. She didn't have coffee but tried it in her strawberry-sugar milk. It was divine! A great way to soak up the last of her second slice of bread.

"That was wonderful," said Jennifer. "Thank you for breakfast."

"You're welcome, dear. Now go change as we'll be leaving soon," replied Harriet.

Jennifer went and quickly put on the navy dress, white socks and flats. When the three of them headed off to church, Harriet wore a navy-blue dress with white polka dots, fitted at the waist and flowing below the knee, a little white hat and white gloves. White button earrings and dress white sandals completed her outfit. Norman wore a dark blue suit with white shirt and dark blue tie.

As Norman drove, Harriet asked, "Did you sleep well after your scare?"

"It took me a long time to go to sleep. I kept worrying about going to the hospital. You know. If I don't remember. I don't want to go to the hospital."

"You're not going to the hospital," said Norman. "What makes you think that?"

"Dr. Baxter said if I can't remember, he would have to admit me for tests."

"Don't you worry about that," said Norman. "I'm sure your memory will be back and you won't have to go at all. After church, we're going on a picnic. We invited Grace along. I'm sure she can help you remember."

"Won't she feel hurt when I can't remember her?"

"No, we called her mom last night after you went to bed and explained. It'll be all right."

Jennifer realized she didn't have to pretend to know Grace. But during the rest of the drive to church, she again worried about whether she should confide in Grace. If she was such a good friend of Julie's, Grace surely would know Jennifer was an impostor. But Julie's parents didn't know; they just thought she couldn't remember. When they pulled up to the church, Jennifer was still trying to decide what to do.

6

Amazing Grace

J ennifer recognized Grace as she came running up to the car. If the long blond hair and blue eyes weren't enough, the hug Grace gave her certainly confirmed this was Julie's best friend. Taking Jennifer totally by surprise, the embrace felt warm and sincere.

Grace finally stepped back and looked at Jennifer.

"Are you all right? When your mom called, she said you fell out of the tree again and couldn't remember anything. You remember me though, right?"

"You're Grace. I'm sorry, but I only know you because of a picture at the house."

A hurt expression flitted across Grace's eyes but was immediately replaced with a look of concern.

"It's OK. I'm coming fishing with you after church. I bet by the time you catch your first fish, you'll remember everything. Can we still sit together in church?"

"Sure, um ... I guess."

What a little church! A small, white church with deep mahogany double doors greeted them. Walking into the entryway, Jennifer noticed a coat bar on one side and a podium holding a guest registry on the other.

Maybe I should sign the guest registry to prove I was here in case I'm suddenly pulled home again. Or, maybe not. That would certainly get me a trip to the hospital.

Grace and Jennifer continued into the sanctuary and her gaze was immediately drawn to two large stained-glass windows. One, a large picture of Jesus teaching children, and the other on the opposite wall, Jesus feeding the multitudes. Each was full of vibrant shades of red, yellow, orange, purple, and green. Bright and beautiful, they depicted the love of Jesus for His followers.

She continued to look around, noticing only seven pews on each side of the aisle. A wooden cross hung over the altar, the pulpit on the left of the altar, and the baptismal font on the right. The furniture was made simply but beautiful in oak wood.

Grace sat in the last pew, Jennifer sliding in beside her. As they settled, the pastor took his place behind the pulpit.

Jennifer sat through the service, trying hard to concentrate. Her mind wandered. When singing "Amazing Grace," she could not stop herself from thinking of Julie's friend, Grace. She knew she wasn't the grace the song talked about, but what if she was? What if God sent this Grace to help her with her present dilemma? She just didn't know if she could trust her.

The pastor led a prayer for people who were hurt or ill, including Julie. Jennifer also prayed for Julie, once again wondering where she could be. If Jennifer was here instead of Julie, was Julie taking her place at home? *Please God, keep Julie safe wherever she is.*

Jennifer knew her parents and Ryan would also be in church, a much larger building made mostly of brick with huge windows to let in the light. It held lots of pews, had carpeted floors, and a large cross hanging over the altar. Hundreds of people attended, most of whom she didn't know at all. *I like this small, intimate church better.*

When the service was over, Grace and Jennifer headed outside while waiting for Norman and Harriet. Jennifer noticed two outhouses behind the church—one for men and one for women—she guessed. She noticed a long building about twenty feet from the church, maybe twenty-five feet wide and forty feet long, also painted white, with windows running along each wall.

"What is that building?" Jennifer asked Grace.

"That's the fellowship hall. That's where we hold dinners for funerals and weddings. And, of course, the pie and ice cream socials."

"Pie and ice cream socials? What's that?"

"You really don't remember anything, do you? That's when all the ladies of the church bring different pies and ice cream. We come and eat. The old folks talk a lot and the kids play. I think maybe it's a fundraiser but I never have to pay. It's loads of fun."

Emerging from the church, Harriet said, "OK, Julie, we're ready to go. Grace, we'll quick go home to change and grab the picnic lunch. We'll pick you up in about forty-five minutes."

* * *

Jennifer popped her last strawberry into her mouth, finishing lunch.

"I can't believe you ate all those strawberries," said Grace. "And not a rash in sight."

"I guess maybe I grew out of that. I'm sure glad. I love them." Grace gave Jennifer a questioning look but said nothing further.

A sunny and warm day, a slight breeze kept them comfortable. The Mississippi River glided gently past them, shimmering in the sunlight.

Jennifer said, "This is a beautiful spot. Where are we?"

"The Mississippi River," replied Norman.

"Yes, I know that, but where? The Mississippi River runs, I think, all the way from upper Minnesota to the Gulf of Mexico."

"You're right about that. You sure remember the oddest things," said

Norman. "We're a short distance from De Soto, Wisconsin, south of La Crosse."

I'll have to google that as soon as I get home. If I get home. No! When I get home.

"Do you remember at all how to fish?" Grace asked Jennifer. "Like how to put the worm on the hook or how to cast?"

"No," Jennifer replied truthfully. Dad had asked her to go fishing with him but she was always too busy. Besides, it sounded too boring to sit around waiting for fish to bite.

"I can't even remember what a fish looks like," Jennifer continued, stone-faced. "Is a fish big or little? Does it fly or swim or what?"

Grace furrowed her brow, staring at her. "You're kidding, right?" she asked.

"Yes, but I really don't kn ... remember how to fish."

"OK, girls. Here you go," said Norman, giving them each a fishing pole and a can of worms to share. "Do you need help, Julie?"

"Maybe, just to remind me how."

"You just take a big fat worm and work it down over the hook, like this, so as much of the hook is hidden as possible."

"Ugh! I don't think I can do that. They're too squiggly."

"Yes, you can. It never bothered you before."

"I don't know. I don't like squiggly things."

"Well, the rule is, whether you remember or not, you have to bait your own hook. This is the last time I'll do it for you."

Norman continued, "Now for the casting. You hold your thumb on this button right here on the reel and bring the pole behind your shoulder, still holding the button down. Make sure there are no people or trees or shrubs in your way before you cast."

Jennifer looked around. They were on the Mississippi River with trees and shrubs everywhere, even trees growing in the river with branches poking up close to shore.

Norman continued. "Then take the pole and bring it forward and when your arm starts the arc toward the river, release the button."

"That sounds pretty complicated. You want me to hold the button down and put the pole back over my shoulder. Then, you want me to swing it forward and let go of the button when I cast toward the river. And you want me to miss all people, trees, and shrubs?"

"You got it!"

As Norman moved over toward Harriet, Jennifer rolled her eyes and looked at Grace.

"You go first. I'll watch you."

Grace had her worm on the hook ready to fish. She brought her pole easily over her shoulder and swung gently toward the river. Her line sailed about thirty feet and landed in a clear spot in the river.

"See? Nothing to it," Grace said with a smile.

"OK. That looks easy." Jennifer took her pole and put her thumb on the button. Checking around for people, trees, and shrubs, she swung the pole behind her shoulder and brought it forward, releasing the button. Her hook landed about two feet in front of her on the sand.

"That doesn't look quite right. Can I catch fish that close to shore?" Jennifer quipped.

"You just held the button too long," said Norman. "Try again."

Jennifer got set again and this time the line dropped behind her shoulder.

"I know. I know," Jennifer giggled. "I let go too soon."

It took Jennifer two more tries and she finally got the line out in the river but it crossed Grace's line.

"Oh, oh. Now what?"

"You just stay there. I'll move over so we won't be crossed." Grace moved to the right, ducking under Jennifer's line and hers pulled away from Jennifer's.

"Now that you finally got your bait in," Grace teased, "watch your red and white bobber. When it moves, you have a nibble. When it dips under the water, pull hard to try and set the hook. Then just reel in your fish."

After about five minutes, Jennifer, already bored, asked "How long does this take?"

"It depends. You haven't waited that long yet. If you get too bored, you could practice casting."

Just then, Grace's bobber started bobbing up and down and finally went completely under.

"Ooh-ooh, I got a bite!" Grace said. She set the hook and started to reel in.

"I've got him. I can feel it." Grace pulled in a nice sunfish.

"He's a keeper," said Norman. He reached for the stringer they had ready to slide the fish on. "First fish of the day. Good job."

"I've got a bite too," Harriet said. As soon as she said it, her bobber went under and she set the hook, pulling in another nice sunfish. Norman took it off the hook and added it to the stringer.

Jennifer watched her bobber with new enthusiasm. In a few minutes, her bobber dipped and she started hopping. "I got a bite! I got a bite!"

"Quit jumping. You'll scare the fish," warned Grace.

Jennifer tried to stand still and be patient. Her bobber went all the way under and she pulled hard. Her hook came loose and went flying over her shoulder, minus the fish.

"I guess I pulled too hard," she said.

"It's OK but your worm is gone for sure," said Norman.

Jennifer looked forlornly at the empty hook. She really did not like squiggly things but if she wanted to catch a fish, she had to put a worm on. Tentatively, she reached into the can of worms and pulled one out. She worked it on the hook as fast as she could and hoped it would stay long enough to catch a fish.

Remembering all the casting tips, Jennifer swung her line about twenty feet into the river.

"I think I've got the hang of this," she said with a grin.

"It's probably coming back to you," replied Harriet. "We've done a lot of fishing."

After a few minutes, Jennifer got another bite and waited patiently for the perfect time to set the hook. As soon as her bobber went under, she pulled gently and could feel the fish on the line.

"I've got one! I've got one!" Jennifer said. She started reeling in and just as the fish got to shore, it flipped off the hook. In her excitement, she ran into the water trying to catch the fish before it got away. Missing, she turned around to see Norman, Harriet, and Grace laughing at her antics. She joined in, laughing along with the others.

"No more! My side hurts," said Jennifer.

"Mine too," Grace said, "but you looked so silly."

They finally went back to fishing, ending with a nice stringer of fish, with Jennifer catching several.

While fishing, Jennifer had been thinking of asking Norman and Harriet if she could have Grace stay overnight. Did they do that way back then, or rather now? Or would that be *way* out of character? They had been having a good time. Like having Paige and Kelly with her. Feeling a twinge of homesickness, she realized she felt close to Grace too.

She might tell Grace the truth if they could be alone. Would it be a mistake? Could it help or would it hurt? Grace could tell her all about Julie's life. If Jennifer couldn't get back home, maybe Grace could tell her enough so Harriet and Norman thought she remembered so she wouldn't have to go to the hospital.

"Time to pack up, girls," said Norman. "I need to get home and do chores."

If ... I mean, when I get home, I'm going to ask Dad to take me fishing with him and Ryan. He would love it.

As they reeled in their lines, removed hooks, and put away their fishing tackle, Jennifer continued to think about Grace and what she should do. Through the afternoon, Norman and Harriet seemed more and more relieved, probably because Jennifer was enjoying herself and seemed to remember how to fish.

What the heck. Here goes. "Would it be OK if Grace came and stayed overnight tonight? We've had such fun I hate to see it end."

"You have chores tomorrow," replied Harriet. "We have to pick garden and probably can some beans."

"We could take her home first thing tomorrow morning," said Jennifer.

"I could stop and get my bike. We could put it in the trunk and I could ride home in the morning. If it's OK with you and my mom."

"It's fine with us if it's fine with her," Norman confirmed.

OK. Grace is coming with us. I just have to decide what to do.

35

7

Show and Tell

Jennifer worried all the way home and through supper about telling Grace the truth. She *needed* to tell someone, someone who would believe her. Grace was the most natural choice. Harriet and Norman didn't believe her and Grace was Julie's best friend. She would soon figure out Jennifer was not Julie. Besides, if Jennifer never got home, she would need to know more about Julie. Grace came home with them, Jennifer told herself, so she could tell her the truth. Getting up the nerve to do so was another matter.

After supper, Norman got ready to milk cows.

Again, putting off the decision, Jennifer asked, "Can Grace and I help at the barn? Maybe we could feed kittens or something. Do you have kittens?"

Three heads turned and looked at her, shock written all over their faces.

"You don't like the barn. You've said that more times than I can count," said Norman.

"Well, but I don't remember *not* liking the barn. Maybe I will like it now."

"If you want to and Grace doesn't mind," replied Norman.

"I don't mind. I love the barn," Grace said.

"Let's go then," said Norman.

As they walked out the door, Pal came from somewhere, running ahead of them. They entered the barnyard through a fence.

"Don't touch the fence, Julie," said Norman. "It's electric."

The fence went as far as could be seen around the pasture.

Jennifer looked with awe at the scene in front of her. From the barn which sat on a hill, she could see for miles. The sky, a deep robin's egg blue, set off the wisps of floating white clouds. Across the landscape, she saw other houses and barns in the distance, along with windmills, silos, and fields and fields of crops. She couldn't believe how many different shades of green she saw in the crops, grasses, and trees, along with golden fields and blooming flowers interspersed. *Enchanting!*

Jennifer turned in a circle trying to take it all in when Grace interrupted, "Watch out for the cow pies."

"What's a cow pie?"

"You know, where the cows go. Those round things there. Some of them are pretty fresh and pretty messy if you step in one."

"They're called cow pies? Oh, I guess because they're round," Jennifer realized. Now that she was aware of them, she did pick up the strong odor, along with another scent.

"What is that sweet smell? Not the cow pies, right?"

"No, of course not. You better not get your nose too close to one of them. The sweet smell is probably the clover. There's a field of it right over there." Grace was pointing to one of the green fields Jennifer had noticed earlier, with little white and lilac flowers throughout. "And there are lots of wildflowers," Grace continued, pointing as she named them. "Wild roses, daisies."

Cows headed in from the pasture, Pal circling around others to herd them toward the barn.

"Wow," said Jennifer. "Pal looks like he's bringing the cows in."

"That's what he does," said Grace. "He's a good cow dog."

Once in the barn, each cow entered a milking stall.

"I wondered how they got a cow to stand still to milk," said Jennifer.

"The stanchions work well," replied Grace. Jennifer and Grace walked in front of the stanchions. A pipe ran from saucer to saucer in front of each cow.

"What are these little dishes for?" asked Jennifer.

"That's so the cows can drink. See, they just push this little knob with their noses." Grace demonstrated. "And water runs into the dish."

"Awesome. Can I touch a cow?"

"Sure. Just move slowly so you don't startle them."

Jennifer put out her hand and petted the head of the cow closest to her. Big brown eyes looked at her without much interest.

"His fur is really coarse."

"It's called hide, cowhide, and it's a girl."

Jennifer noticed Norman getting ready to milk. She nodded toward him and said, "Let's watch."

"OK, if you want to."

Norman was at the far end of the barn away from the door. He took a three-legged stool and placed it on the right side of the cow, sat down, and with a cloth washed each of the four teats and the udder of the cow. He then placed a pail between his knees and began to milk.

Jennifer watched for a while in fascination.

"Doesn't it hurt them?" she asked.

"No. Their udders are full of milk. As the milk is released, the pressure lessens."

Once milked, Norman released each cow from its stanchion and it ambled back outside.

"Can I try it?" Jennifer asked.

"If you want to," replied Norman, sounding surprised. "Just sit down here." As she did, Norman continued, "Now wash her good before you start." When Jennifer had washed the cow as instructed, Norman added, "Now take two teats at a time, one in each hand. Pull and squeeze gently but firmly until you get milk into the pail."

Jennifer tried but could get no milk.

"You're being a little too gentle. Squeeze and pull at the same time. You'll get it."

At the next try, Jennifer squeezed some milk into the pail.

"I did it! I got milk!" Jennifer said. "This is so fun." Jennifer milked until her hands tired and Norman took over again.

"You did a really good job," said Norman. "I'm proud of you."

Jennifer glowed.

"Do you girls want to feed the cats now?" asked Norman.

"Sure," they answered.

"There's some milk I kept separate over by the milk cans by the door. Pour a little in the cats' bowl. The rest can go to the calves. I'm sure Grace can show you how," he added when he saw Jennifer's hesitation.

Jennifer and Grace started toward the front of the barn.

"Look out!" yelled Grace.

"What?" Alarmed, Jennifer turned to Grace.

"Hurry! Move!"

Jennifer jumped toward Grace, following her line of vision. It was then Jennifer noticed a cow, tail raised, going to the bathroom. A gutter about eighteen inches wide and six inches deep ran the full length of the barn behind the cows. Jennifer had noticed it before but didn't know its purpose. Even though the cow hit the gutter, the splash went everywhere, just missing Jennifer.

"Thanks. That was close."

"It would have been funnier if you had gotten splashed," said Grace, grinning, "but under the circumstances, I thought I should warn you."

"You're all heart."

Grace and Jennifer continued to feed the animals.

"Where are the kittens?" asked Jennifer as she poured milk into a bowl. "I want to hold one."

"They won't let you. They're barn cats and too wild. They eat only when we're not around. Remember the gray kitten we tried to catch one time I stayed over? That scratch took a while to heal. Let's feed the calves."

The girls found four calves of various sizes. While petting their heads, they each held a bucket of milk for a calf to drink.

"They're so cute and hungry," said Jennifer. One calf's enthusiasm almost caused her to lose the bucket.

"Yeah. They get fed twice a day but they act like it's been a week."

One of the calves found Jennifer's hand and started sucking on it.

"His tongue feels like sandpaper. It's so rough."

They spent quite a bit of time feeding and petting the calves. Jennifer wondered if she should go ahead and tell Grace now, while they were alone. Or were they too close to Norman? Could he hear them?

As they continued to pet the calves, Jennifer looked at the barn around her. She had seen most of the ground floor and wondered aloud, "What's upstairs?"

"The hayloft. That's where the hay is stored that's been baled for the cows to eat when there's no grass, like in winter."

"Can we go see it?" asked Jennifer.

"I guess."

They climbed a built-in ladder leading to the hayloft. Jennifer's first peek over the edge surprised her. Hay bales piled high gave off a sweet pungent aroma.

"Wow. That's a lot of hay," said Jennifer.

"There'll be lots more soon. Some of this is last year's crop. You can tell by how old they look. The newer bales are more gold and the older ones browner. Your dad will have one more crop, probably in August, to add to this. It needs to last all winter."

Jennifer thought this might be the perfect place to tell Grace. It should be far enough away from Norman.

"Can we go up?" asked Jennifer.

"Sure, just climb up."

Jennifer and Grace climbed into the hayloft and Jennifer looked around. She saw two bales just inside the door and sat down.

"Grace ... I need to ... talk to you ... about something," started Jennifer, her hands sweaty and her voice shaky.

"Girls, time to go," called Norman.

"Oh, he's done milking? That was fast," said Jennifer. "We'll be right down."

"What did you want to talk about?" Grace asked.

"It'll wait. We'd better go."

Norman had put four milk cans on a little cart with two wheels. He pushed the cart to the milk house, Grace and Jennifer following behind.

When the girls entered the kitchen, Harriet said, "I thought you girls would be back long ago. I've been feeling like a game of Chinese Checkers. Are you up for it?"

"Do you want to?" Jennifer asked Grace.

"I don't care, but you said ..." started Grace.

Interrupting, Jennifer said, "Sure. Sounds like fun."

Harriet set up the game.

"What color marbles do you girls want?" she asked.

"Green," replied Jennifer.

"Yellow," said Grace.

"OK, let's stagger them. Since there are six colors and only three of us, let's do every other color. Do you remember how?" asked Grace.

"No," replied Jennifer. "Remind me."

"We put all our marbles in our space and try to get them to the opposite side before the other players. You can jump your own marbles or someone else's, like checkers. The more you can jump in a row, the faster you'll get there."

"OK. Let's play. I'll get it."

The three of them played two games, with Grace winning the first game and Jennifer winning the second.

"That's enough for me," said Harriet. "I think I'll watch a little television."

Grace looked at Jennifer expectantly. Jennifer knew what she was thinking.

"We're going to go out and sit for a while," said Jennifer. "We'll be right outside."

They walked outside and around the house. Jennifer took possession of the tree swing and Grace sat on a big rock under the tree. Enough light was coming from the living room window so Jennifer could watch Grace's eyes. *OK, here goes.*

"I want to tell you something, but you have to promise, *promise* you won't tell anyone else."

"OK, I promise."

"It's very important you don't tell anyone, not even your mom and dad."

"OK."

"You may not believe me and I don't know how to explain it, but ..."

"Just say it. How bad can it be?"

Jennifer finally blurted out the story, knowing it didn't make sense, and anyone in their right mind wouldn't believe it.

"I know this is going to sound crazy, but it's true. I'm not Julie. I didn't fall out of a tree and lose my memory. I'm Jennifer. I was pulled into my bathroom mirror at home, in 2009, and ended up here in 1958 and everyone thinks I'm Julie, but I'm not."

Grace looked at her like she was insane.

8

Hurt Feelings

Grace said, "I know. Not who you are or where you came from, but I *know* you're not Julie."

Jennifer could not believe her ears. "How? How could you know?"

"I just do. Julie loves to fish and doesn't mind putting worms on the hook. Even if she didn't remember, she still wouldn't mind, would she? And, she hates the barn. You seemed to enjoy all of it. But most of all, when Julie eats strawberries, she gets hives all over her body. She *never* eats strawberries."

"Then why don't Julie's parents know? They've been with me the whole time."

"They can't believe something like that could happen. I can't explain it but I know you're not Julie. Where is Julie?"

"I don't know. I've thought about her and prayed she's safe. Maybe she's at my house."

"Was Julie in the darkness too? Did you see anything?"

"No. She could have been two inches from me and I still wouldn't have seen her. Everything was black. And I couldn't hear anything either. That could have been because I was screaming. It feels so good

43

to tell someone who believes me. *Please* don't tell anyone. I'm so afraid of being taken to the hospital because they think I'm crazy."

"I promise. Maybe we should try to figure out what happened. Think of some way to get you home."

"How can we do that?"

"You said you saw Julie in your mirror and just touched it. Maybe if we look in the mirror, she'll be waiting."

"I hadn't thought of that. Let's try."

They went into the house going directly to Julie's room and sat at her dresser.

"I don't see anything, but maybe if I touch the mirror it will just happen."

Jennifer turned to Grace.

"If I do go, I want to thank you for being my friend. I know you want Julie back." Jennifer hugged Grace this time. "It was really fun and I'll always remember you."

"You too, Jennifer. I wish I could have both of you."

Jennifer turned back to the mirror. Her hand shaking, she reached out, but pulled back again. Closing her eyes, she inhaled and slowly let out her breath. *Please God, let this work.* She opened her eyes and reached out again. Touching the mirror, she felt only cool glass. She moved her hand around. Up and down, back and forth. Nothing happened. Disappointed that she was not going home, tears came to Jennifer's eyes.

Seeing her distress, Grace put her arm around Jennifer's shoulder. "I'm sorry. I know how much you want to go home. What time did this happen? Maybe it has to be that time."

"It was, I guess, about five yesterday afternoon. Maybe if I try again tomorrow about that time?"

"You could try. I don't have any other ideas. Since you don't seem to be going anywhere real soon, tell me about your life. Is it a lot different than here?"

"It's *way* different. For one thing, I live in a city with about forty thousand people. We have a nice house with *indoor* plumbing. We have two cars, three TVs, a computer. And cell phones. Lots of people have cell phones now instead of the one phone like here."

"What's a computer and what's a cell phone?"

"A computer is like a typewriter, but better. Do you have typewriters?"

"Yes. Of course, we have typewriters."

"OK. A computer is sort of like a typewriter, but you can do lots more. You can type on it and save it and then print it out later or change it and save it again. You can also play games on it and you can find out stuff on the Internet."

"What's an Internet?"

"That's part of the computer. You can go into Google or Yahoo and find out all sorts of stuff, like geography or science or history. You can even shop over the Internet."

"How can you shop? How can you get stuff through a machine?"

"You just click on something you want to buy, give them your credit card number, and they mail it."

"What's a credit card?"

"That's a little card, like a driver's license, with a personalized number. You give them that number for payment, they mail the item you ordered, and the credit card bills you."

"Wow! That's amazing! So, what's a cell phone?"

"It's a phone but hand-held. It's little and lots of people carry one with them all the time. Sometimes for emergencies. They can play games on them too and text people."

"Text?"

"That's when you type messages to friends or family instead of talking to them."

"Why wouldn't you just talk to them?"

"It's more fun to text. Everyone is doing it. Except me. I don't have a cell phone. You can do all sorts of things with cell phones besides talk."

"Wow! Maybe we should write down what our life is like. You write down what happened and what your life is like and I can write down what my life is like and then we'll trade. If you do get home, you'll have something from me and I'll have something from you."

"That's a great idea. When I do get home, I can look at the note and know I wasn't crazy and it wasn't just a weird dream."

They spent a lot of time asking each other questions and making notes about the differences in their lives.

About done, Jennifer asked Grace, "What's a chamber pot? Harriet told me last night I should have used the chamber pot instead of going to the outhouse."

"Oh. That's the little pot under your bed, for going to the bathroom at night."

Jennifer looked. Sure enough, a little round, white metal pot with a red rim and a handle on the side was under the bed. About nine inches in diameter and eight inches high, it looked too small to sit on.

"You really use that?"

"Sure, especially when it's cold or raining."

"This gets crazier and crazier. You really sit on that?"

Grace's face turned red. Her eyes filled with tears. "This is my life and I love it," she snapped. "You're so used to having everything. *Indoor plumbing*, two cars, zillions of televisions and computers. Don't use the chamber pot. Go outside and be attacked by bats again."

Jennifer looked at Grace, astonished at her reaction.

Harriet poked her head in the bedroom, "Girls, it's time for bed. Julie has work to do tomorrow."

"OK. We're just finishing up," replied Jennifer.

Jennifer and Grace got ready for bed in silence. Jennifer didn't want to deal with the outhouse, bats, or the chamber pot so she crawled into bed. Grace came to bed a few minutes later.

"Good night, Grace."

Grace didn't answer.

Jennifer again lay awake for a long time. *Did I really hurt Grace's feelings? Will she stay mad? Tell her mom and dad what I told her? I better apologize first thing in the morning.*

***

"Girls," said Harriet from the doorway of the bedroom, "time to get up. I let you sleep a little longer but now it's time to move."

Jennifer and Grace slowly crawled out of bed. Grace looked as tired as Jennifer felt. *Maybe Grace didn't sleep well either.*

"Here," said Grace, handing Jennifer her letter. "I need to get home right away. It's late."

Jennifer took the letter and went to get hers to give Grace. Before she could retrieve it, Grace was gone.

Jennifer put Grace's letter in her jean pocket. She wanted it with her at all times, in case she was pulled home.

As Jennifer walked into the kitchen, Harriet said, "Grace just left and wouldn't even stay for breakfast. Are you two OK?"

"Um, we had a little misunderstanding. It was my fault. I said something that hurt her feelings, I guess. I need to call her and apologize."

"I can't imagine what you could have said to make her mad at you. She won't be home yet and I know they were going away today. You might have to wait to call later tonight."

After a quick bowl of cereal, Harriet and Jennifer headed to the garden. Harriet pulled a wagon with ten galvanized pails set inside.

"That's a lot of pails. What do we have to do in the garden?"

"We may not need them all. While it's still cool, we need to pick cucumbers, green beans, and strawberries. Maybe weed a little. We'll start with the cucumbers," Harriet said as she handed Jennifer a pail and

47

bent over to start picking. "We need to pick from about two inches and longer. They hide under the vines so look carefully."

"Why such different sizes?"

"The little ones will be for midget dill pickles. There won't be enough today, but we'll wash them and keep them until the next picking. The larger ones we'll eat fresh or I'll slice them and make dill spears."

"What are these green things on this bush?"

"They're tomatoes. They just haven't ripened yet. Some people like fried green tomatoes, but we'd rather wait until they're red."

Next, they picked green beans three to four inches long, filling five four-quart pails. Jennifer again learned to look carefully in the bushes, pushing the leaves aside gently to find the beans.

As Jennifer picked, she thought of Grace. She hadn't meant to hurt her feelings. But everything was so different. She also thought about trying the mirror again at five. Would it work? Of course, she didn't know the *exact* time. But she hoped it worked. If she didn't get home soon, she feared she might end up in the hospital one way or another. *I have to get home. I just have to!*

Jennifer pulled herself back to the present, picking beans.

"What are you going to do with all these beans?" Jennifer asked.

"I'll can some today. I have some left from the last picking and we'll probably have some for supper. How does fresh green beans sound?"

"Wonderful."

They took a break and Jennifer again marveled at the beauty around her. Another beautiful day but the hard work had them both sweating. Unlike working in her flower garden, she couldn't just quit when she felt like it. The vegetables needed picking or they would get too big or too ripe and be wasted. *If I ever get home, I still want to ask Dad if I can try a little vegetable garden.*

After resting, they picked strawberries. They moved the leaves gently back and forth, the red berries easier to see than the green beans and cucumbers. But still a lot of work.

By the time they were done picking, Jennifer was hot, sweaty, tired, and in need of a cool drink. They filled the wagon with pails of produce, carried some, and started toward the house. When they reached the yard, Jennifer pumped a dipper of water for Harriet from the outside pump and then one for herself. She marveled again at the flow of water.

"Thank you, Julie. That tastes good. It got hot early today," said Harriett.

They went into the kitchen, washed their hands, and Harriet took out a large bowl. Copying Harriet, Jennifer snapped off the stem end of the beans, snapped them in smaller pieces, and put them in the bowl.

Getting up from the table, Harriet said, "I'll start getting the jars ready."

Jennifer continued snapping beans while Harriet sterilized seven glass quart jars. Putting them in a big, dark blue pot with white spots all over, she poured hot water over everything until the water filled the canner and jars so they were just covered. When the water started to boil, Harriett lifted the jars carefully with a grabber and emptied the hot water back into the pot. Next, she filled the sterilized jars with washed beans, shook them down to pack them, added a little salt, and covered them with water. The lids, which had been soaking in boiling water, were laid on top of the jars, screwed on tightly with the bands, and put back into the pot. When all seven were in the canner, Harriet put it on the stove, and turned the burner on high.

"How long will it take to cook them?" Jennifer asked.

"Once they come to a boil, about three hours."

"It sure is a lot of work."

"It'll be worth it this winter when we're eating freshly canned garden beans. And we still have plenty left for supper tonight. Your dad will be in soon so we need to get the table set. Would you please cut a few of the bigger cucumbers to go with lunch?"

Later, Jennifer and Harriet started on the strawberries. They pulled

49

the stems out and put the berries into a bowl for washing.

"Are you going to can these too?" asked Jennifer, popping a strawberry in her mouth.

"No. It's late in the season so there aren't enough. We'll eat the last few fresh. I still can't understand why you aren't getting hives from them. Maybe you did grow out of that."

When they had a bowl full of berries, Harriet poured cool water over them and gently washed them. She transferred the berries from one bowl to another, washed them again, and put them in the refrigerator.

For Jennifer the time seemed to drag. Too early before she could try the mirror or phone Grace, Jennifer asked, "Is there something else I can help with?"

"Thank you. I think you've done enough today. You just relax."

Jennifer didn't want to relax. The work might help keep her mind off of home.

"You said something about weeding. Can I do that?" asked Jennifer.

"If you want to weed tomatoes, there's a hoe around the corner in the shed."

Jennifer headed outside and called for Pal. He came running up to her, now used to her scent. Jennifer found a stick, threw it for him, and he took off at a run, bringing it back to her in a flash. She threw it farther the next time and while he was gone, she found the hoe. She threw the stick a few more times.

"Come on, boy. We're going to do a little hoeing."

Jennifer began weeding the tomatoes, working with her hands when too close to the plants for hoeing.

While she worked, she thought about her family. It was Monday and Mom would be at her job at the hospital and her dad at his law practice. Was he in court today? He got pretty intense when he had to be in court. Jennifer wished she was home taking care of Ryan. That was her job and she missed being there. She liked playing games with him, like

Checkers or Trouble. Or playing marbles. He liked marbles a lot and was getting pretty good at it. *I really miss him. I really miss all of them. I hope the mirror works when I try again.* Once again hot and sweaty, her hands had blisters from hoeing. She thought it must be close to five. She needed to get back, call Grace to apologize, and try the mirror. When Jennifer returned to the house, she realized she had been out longer than she thought. If she wanted to try the mirror at five, she'd better not call Grace. She took her letter written earlier and added an apology. She put Grace's name on the outside, signed it 'J', then put it in a spot sure to be found.

Jennifer sat down at the mirror and took a deep breath. Closing her eyes, she said a silent prayer. It had to be very close to the time she had been sent here. It was now or never. Opening her eyes, she reached out, her hand shaking. As she touched the mirror . . .

9

Wash Day

Nothing. Nada. Zip. Not a quiver. Again, Jennifer felt only cool glass. Frustrated, tears ran down her cheeks. *I guess it was worth a try. I better get hold of Grace.*

"Can I get Grace's number now?" Jennifer asked, walking into the living room.

"Sure. Her number is R48. They might be back by now."

"What kind of a number is that? I need her telephone number."

"That is her telephone number," replied Harriet, giving Jennifer a strange look.

This might be easier if I would learn to keep my mouth shut.

"Pick up the phone," Harriet continued, "dial zero and give the operator that number. She'll connect you. I'll give you some privacy." She put her book down and headed for the kitchen.

Jennifer picked up the phone and dialed zero as instructed.

"Operator. May I help you?"

Jennifer gave the number and heard ringing on the other end. She let it ring numerous times and finally hung up.

She went in and lay down on Julie's bed, her arm across her eyes. Two sleepless nights, lots of exercise, and the added stress had her close to crying. *Please God. Please help me. I don't know how this happened or why. And I don't know what to do.*

Poking her head through the doorway, Harriet said, "Are you all right? Did you get hold of Grace?"

"No. They weren't home yet. I'm OK. Just really tired."

"You pushed yourself too much today. After supper, you better relax."

That's exactly what Jennifer did. After supper, she took the foot basin again and washed. She thought about the long soothing showers she took at home, never once thanking God for that simple pleasure. *Thank you, God. I'm sorry I didn't thank you before for all you've given me. I know I'm blessed with all I have. Please, please, help me get back home.* She then donned pajamas and headed out to watch TV. She could hardly wait to see what they were watching tonight.

Gunsmoke, an old Western. It moved so slowly. She could do her homework in front of this show and never miss a thing. Better than *The Lawrence Welk Show*. Still boring.

The commercials for Marlboro cigarettes bothered her. Why did they advertise for something so bad for people? She knew if she voiced her thought she would get another of those "looks."

"What are we doing tomorrow?" Jennifer asked Harriet.

"We need to wash clothes. It's supposed to be another nice day."

Jennifer wanted to try Grace's number again even though she would have no privacy.

"Do you mind if I try Grace again?" asked Jennifer.

"No dear, go ahead," replied Harriet.

Jennifer picked up the phone, remembered to dial zero and gave the operator Grace's number. After two rings, someone answered.

"Hello."

"Hello. Is Grace there?"

"This is me."

"Oh, Grace. I'm glad I reached you. This is Je … Julie. I wanted to apologize for last night. I didn't mean to hurt your feelings."

"I'm sorry, too. I know this is all new to you and it must be hard. I shouldn't have gotten mad."

"We're OK then?"

"Yes. We're OK. Did you try the mirror? "

"Yes. I guess I better go. I just needed to apologize."

"OK. Bye. And good luck."

After a while, Jennifer said good-night to Harriet and Norman and headed to bed. She was having a hard time concentrating on TV anyway, such as it was. She was too tired and dejected to sit and relax. *What are Mom and Dad watching? Do they even know I'm gone?*

At least she didn't have to worry about Grace telling her secret. Grace said they were OK and Jennifer believed her. Pretty soon, though, Harriet would want her to see the doctor because of her memory loss. Remembering the heat from the night before, Jennifer opened the window, crawled into bed, and cried herself to sleep. Exhausted, she finally slept without the worry of the past few days.

She woke the next morning refreshed, sunshine again pouring in the window. She heard the happy twill of a bird's song from the tree just outside. A cool breeze washed over her, making the curtains flutter and the leaves glimmer in the sunlight. *What a gorgeous day!* Filled with new hope, she climbed out of bed and dressed in blue-jean shorts and an orange short sleeve top.

Even though she was up early, Harriet and Norman were already in the kitchen. They stopped talking when she entered.

"Good morning. How are you doing this morning?" asked Norman. "You looked pretty tired last night."

"I was. I'm ready for a new day. I forgot. What are we doing?"

"It's Tuesday, wash day," said Harriet.

Tuesday. Mom and Dad are at work. Who will take care of Ryan? Is Julie there with him? Would she know how to play with a little boy to keep him entertained and keep him safe?

After breakfast, Jennifer helped Harriet set up the washing machine and tubs on the side porch. An old-fashioned machine with a wringer Jennifer had seen in pictures. Two rinse tubs came next followed by a laundry basket on a chair, forming a circle. With Jennifer's help, Harriet filled the two tubs with cold water pumped from the outside pump and hauled in. They sorted the clothes in piles, dark clothes, light clothes, whites. Lastly, Harriet filled the washing machine with water that had been heated on the stove.

Harriet poured some blue liquid in the last rinse.

"What is that? You didn't use very much."

"That's bluing. It helps keep the white things white and it doesn't take very much. If it gets spilled, you have blue over everything."

When they were ready to start, Harriet said to Jennifer, "I know you don't remember this so I want you to be especially careful. The wringer is very tight. When we put the clothes through, use this pole," showing Jennifer a round dowel about one inch in diameter and eighteen inches long. "You use *this* to put clothes in between the two rollers, not your hands. You should be OK, but if your shirt gets caught, hit this release and it will pop open." Harriet showed Jennifer a release on top of the wringer. She hit it hard with the palm of her hand and it snapped open.

"OK. I'll be careful."

Harriet and Jennifer started with a load of white clothes. Because the water was hot, as they dropped the clothes in the washer, Harriet pushed them under with the pole.

After the first load was washed, Harriet showed Jennifer how to put them through the wringer. She took the pole and brought up a T-shirt and guided it between the rollers. Harriet showed Jennifer how to open up the shirt as it came through the wringer on the other side so it could rinse thoroughly. When the first batch had been transferred to the rinse tub, Harriet swung the wringer around so the clothes would drop into

55

a second rinse tub. Moving the wringer again, the clothes were put through one last time where they dropped into the basket on the chair.

"Now what?" asked Jennifer.

"Now we go hang them out to dry."

Harriet grabbed the basket and gave Jennifer two sacks full of clothespins to carry. They walked around the side of the house to the clotheslines Jennifer had noticed the first night. Harriet put the basket down and took one of the sacks of clothespins, slipping the loop over her head for easy access. Jennifer hung her sack around her neck also. Harriett grabbed a sheet from the basket, Jennifer taking the other end, and they worked the sheet over the line, attaching it with clothespins. Working together, it didn't take long to hang their first basket of laundry.

Jennifer enjoyed the whole wash day process, especially hanging clothes. Bright sunshine and the light breeze would dry them quickly. She could smell the tiger lilies spotted earlier, not far from where they worked. Hummingbirds gathering nectar and rabbits hopping across the yard added to the delight of the day. Jennifer laughed as Pal tried to catch the bunnies but missed every time. She liked the peacefulness, not hurried but a steady working together. *I wonder if I would enjoy this as much if it was my normal life.*

Jennifer's mom did most of the laundry at home with Jennifer helping sometimes. A lot faster and easier with the automatic washer and dryer but not like working together. Nothing serene about it, not like hanging out clothes and enjoying the peaceful beauty around her.

Harriet and Jennifer headed back to the house. The second load would be ready soon since Harriet started it before they went to hang the first load.

Jennifer thought they worked together easily but she didn't know how Harriet and Julie did. Maybe Julie didn't like wash day or maybe they sang or talked a lot. Jennifer didn't say much. Better that way than to say something that would get her in trouble.

It seemed Harriet had read Jennifer's thoughts when she said, "I know this scares you. But your dad and I think we might have to call Dr. Baxter. We think your memory should have come back by now, or at least some of it. You seem to be doing fine otherwise, but we're worried about you."

This was the moment Jennifer had dreaded. Her heart jumped to her throat. Wiping her sweaty hands on her shorts, she said, "No, please. I'm sure it will be OK. I just need some more time."

"We'll see. I'm going to call Dr. Baxter after lunch and at least talk to him about it. We'll see what he says, if it usually takes this long for memory to come back."

They were on their last load, jeans. Harriet asked if Jennifer wanted to hang them or empty the tubs. She showed Jennifer the plugs in the bottom of the tubs and how to empty them into a pail. Even though Jennifer liked hanging clothes, she thought she could try emptying the washing machine and tubs. Her mind had been in turmoil ever since Harriet said she was going to call the doctor.

Harriet headed out to the clotheslines with the last load to hang. Jennifer slid a pail under the first tub and pulled the plug. As the pail filled with water, Jennifer's mind wandered. Even though hard work, she liked this farm life, this simpler life. She liked picking vegetables and strawberries. She liked washing clothes, especially hanging them out to dry. She loved being outdoors. The beauty amazed her; the many shades of green, beautiful flowers everywhere, clear blue sky with fluffy clouds now and then. She appreciated the smell of clean air, the hot sun blazing down, and the gentle breeze cooling her. The clothes smelled wonderful from drying outside.

It felt good to accomplish something in a relaxed way without being in a rush. Mom and Dad were always in a hurry. They hurried to get to work and Mom hurried home to get a meal started because everyone was hungry. Dad hardly ever relaxed. He seemed to be at work more than he was home. She liked working together, picking and canning vegetables. Home grown vegetables tasted great and the fresh strawberries wonderful. Remembering what she was doing, she quickly replaced the plug on the tub. She almost overfilled the pail in her daydreaming. She hauled the water to throw outside and came back to begin the process again.

When Jennifer reached into the tub to pull the plug, she thought she saw Julie in the reflection of the water. She felt a sudden tug on her arm. Screaming, she pulled back with all her strength, but the force was intense. Bracing her feet against the tub for leverage, she pushed hard. It didn't work. She wanted to go home, but not like this! This was water! She didn't want to be dragged into water! How could she breathe? She had no control!

Before her head went into the water, Jennifer yelled, "Julie! Call Grace!"

Jennifer didn't know if Julie heard her or if she would be coming home. Just before her face hit water, she took a deep breath and closed her eyes tightly. Dragged into the tub, she once again felt nothing. *This doesn't feel like water.* She opened her eyes. All was black, as before. No light. No sound. She began spinning, closed her eyes again, and waited for the fall. And waited.

10

Back Again

Jennifer kept her eyes closed, preparing for impact. *I hope I land on my soft bed.* Eager to be home, it seemed to be taking longer than the first time to "fall out." Just before she opened her eyes to take a peek, she hit hard, as before. *Not my soft bed.* While trying to catch her breath, she kept her eyes closed. Thank God she was home.

Opening her eyes, she saw a woman running toward her. She had graying, dark brown hair pulled back in a bun, loose strands hanging around her face and neck. She wore a light blue-and-white-checked dress, faded almost beyond color, a tattered blue bonnet tied under her chin, and laced, brown shoes.

The woman knelt beside Jennifer. Concern shadowed her brown eyes along with a deep weariness. Her face was thin, tanned dark, her nose straight, and her mouth set in a firm line.

"Josie, are you all right?" asked the woman.

Jennifer looked at her. It was happening again! She was *not* home. Now where? Tears came to her eyes, along with a feeling of deep frustration and dread.

"Where am I? Who am I?" Jennifer asked.

The woman stared at her but didn't answer. Her obvious concern changed to apprehension. She quickly turned, searching for something or someone.

Jennifer looked around. She had fallen on a dirt road, bumpy and dusty. It looked like an old town, only two blocks long. Store fronts lined both sides of the street. Mason's Mercantile. Arnie's Blacksmith. Helds's Butcher. Millie's Diner. Several horses stood tied to railings, and others pulled wagons down the street. No cars.

A few onlookers milled around. One came forward. The man, thin and tall, had a long lean face, again dark from the sun. He wore Levi jeans, work boots, and a faded, blue work shirt. Walking fast, with a prominent limp, his black eyes snapped with impatience. "For Pete's sake, Clara," said the man, "git her out of the road."

"Wait," said the woman tentatively. "She could be hurt."

"She's not hurt, just got the wind knocked out of her."

Jennifer realized she must now be Josie. She said again, "Where am I?"

The man's gaze flew to Jennifer. "Don't you go pulling your foolishness on me, young lady. You know dang well where you are. Now git up."

"Clyde, she probably bumped her head. She took quite a spill," said Clara.

Through clenched teeth, he said, "We still got to git her out of the road!"

Jennifer raised on her elbows, her body aching. Her head spun. She slowly rose to her feet with Clara's help. Jennifer now wore a faded calico dress, oxfords, and a bonnet.

"If you hadn't been woolgathering, you would have seen the runaway wagon," Clyde snarled. "We don't have time for your carelessness."

"I'm sorry. I didn't mean to," said Jennifer, cringing.

"You're always sorry, *after*. Why don't you think? Now, let's finish up and git home."

Clara guided Jennifer to Mason's Mercantile, sitting her on a bench inside the door.

"Now, stay put," said Clara. "I'll finish the shopping while Pa is at the blacksmith. Then we can get you home."

Looking around, Jennifer saw a large room with wood plank walls and a wooden floor, scuffed from years of foot traffic. With only the door and one window in front, it was hard to see. As her eyes adjusted to the dim light, she noticed many shelves filled with everything imaginable. She could hardly take it all in. Every conceivable spot held things to buy. On shelves. On tables. On the floor. Even hanging from the ceiling.

One section overflowed with clothes: coveralls, jeans, shirts, socks, gloves, hats, boots, shoes. Another spot had sewing items: fabric, buttons, thread, rolls and rolls of brightly colored ribbon. Then, she saw school supplies: pencils, rulers, books.

Cooking utensils were next: tin plates, bowls, cups, silverware, cast iron pots, and pans hanging from the ceiling. And canning equipment: jars, canners, jar grabbers, lids.

In the back of the store, hardware and tools: hammers, axes, pails, rope, hoes, shovels and open barrels of bulk seeds.

A man scooped nails from a keg. With a three-pronged claw, he grabbed a bunch of nails and put them in a pail on the left of a scale. A one-pound weight sat on the right of the scale and when he reached even weight, he had a pound of nails. Jennifer had never seen nails bought in bulk before.

Items of every sort hung from the ceiling: halters, lanterns. Many things Jennifer didn't recognize.

Two old men sat in wooden rocking chairs playing checkers.

In the front of the store she saw a long counter with a glass case filled with knives, watches, and trinkets of all sorts. On top sat large jars of candy. In addition to the shelves stacked with cans of food, there were also crocks or kegs of food: coffee, flour, sugar, tea, rice, pickles, dried fruit and nuts. Jennifer watched as Clara filled a bag with coffee from a large keg and from a barrel, flour. *Lots of groceries must have been sold in bulk back in these days, whatever these days are.*

Behind the counter, tobacco products lined the wall.

In a corner in front of the store, a woman received mail from a clerk in the tiniest post office Jennifer had ever seen.

On the floor next to Jennifer sat an odd metal bucket, stained brown, she hadn't noticed before. Just then, a man spat a great wad into the spittoon. Jennifer gagged, moved away, and approached Clara.

"How are you feeling?" Clara asked.

"Dizzy and sore."

"Just a few minutes and I'll be done."

"I'm going outside to get some air."

"Stay by the door. We'll be leaving soon."

Jennifer walked out into the fresh air and sat on a wooden bench. Several people walked by.

"Hey, Josie," said a boy coming up to her. "I heard you got hit by a runaway wagon. Are you all right?"

Jennifer looked at the boy with curiosity. A little taller than she, about age twelve, she thought. He wore Levi jeans, work boots, and a light tan shirt. His blue eyes, bright with mischief, fit with his unruly, auburn hair. Freckles sprinkled his wide nose.

"I'm OK. I guess I didn't see the wagon coming."

"You're always daydreaming. I'm surprised you haven't been hit before."

Clara came out of the store, carrying several packages. "Hello, Cecil. How are you today?"

"I'm fine, Mrs. McKinley. Can I help you with your packages?"

"Thank you, Cecil. That would be nice. There are some heavier ones in the store, if you would be so kind."

It didn't take Cecil long to haul the wooden boxes to their wagon. Jus as he loaded the last one, Clyde walked up.

"Jo, why is Cecil doing your chores? You should be helping your ma with these supplies."

Timidly, Clara answered, "Cecil offered and I accepted. Josie is still feeling dizzy from her fall."

"If she wasn't scatterbrained, she wouldn't need someone else to do her chores. We don't need outside help!"

This man is rude to everyone! "You're supposed to be my father? Why are you so mean?"

Clyde stared at Jennifer. His face turned red and he opened his mouth to speak. Seeing Cecil still hovering, he clamped his mouth shut.

Through gritted teeth, he said, "Git in the wagon! We're going home."

Clara gave Cecil an apologetic look and helped Jennifer into the wagon.

Would it do her any good to tell them she was not Josie? She thought not. The man already scared her and now she had called him mean. *What will happen to me now?*

11

Hard Times

The three headed out of town, following a rough road sandwiched between forest-covered bluffs. Soon after they left town, Jennifer felt the incline leading up from the much greener valley. She held on tight as the road began to rise steeply, going around sharp curves. Her attention was drawn to several majestic bald eagles drifting on the wind currents, blue sky background to their brown bodies and white heads. She heard the cawing of crows as the wagon rattled down the uneven road. The clip-clop of horses' hooves sent dust flying in their faces already streaked with perspiration and dirt. She wished for a breeze, even though it would create more dust. No one spoke.

At the top of the bluff, the road evened out. The terrain flattened into gently rolling hills and fields with early crops of corn, hay, and tobacco. *This reminds me of the land by the farm.* Half an hour later, a small, unpainted farmhouse and dilapidated barn came into Jennifer's view.

She noticed three cows fenced in behind the barn and a few chickens pecking in the dirt. A bedraggled garden was on one side of the house, with a well in between the garden and barn. A small shed sat next to the house and what looked like the dreaded outhouse farther back.

Please, God. Don't let this be Josie's home.

Oh no! Clyde stopped the wagon in front of the house. Clara helped Jennifer down while Clyde heaved a large feed bag out of the wagon.

He said, "Jo, you help your ma take in the supplies and then git to your chores. You need to finish that garden."

Jennifer did not answer. She took a wooden box, heavier than it looked, and struggled as she went inside. She found herself in a small room with log walls and a pine plank floor. On one wall stood a black stove with a rustic box of chopped wood beside it. It reminded her of the logs her dad bought for their fireplace at home.

She set the box on a rough table surrounded by three wooden chairs. Next to the door, three large nails held coats and hats. Two of the walls had two shelves each starting halfway up the wall. One spot held food: flour, sugar, coffee, items they had purchased in town. On the next shelf she saw an assortment of pans, tin plates, bowls, and cups, one holding silverware. It looked like just enough for three people to eat a meal.

A small table held a dish pan for washing hands like the one on the farm and a short shelf next to it held odds and ends: matches, soap, toothbrushes.

On the other side of the room, she spied a curtained-off section and wondered what was behind the curtain. A homemade wooden ladder led up to a loft.

This is so small, hardly room to move around the room. How do three people live and work in this space? Our house is way bigger than this for four of us.

After a quick scan of the room, Jennifer went out to get another box. She would have liked to lie down somewhere. She still felt dizzy and her head hurt. She knew resting was not an option.

Jennifer brought another box into the house. "I'm sorry. I really can't remember. I must have hit my head hard in the fall."

Clara looked at her again with growing concern. "I can tell you don't recollect. We have to try and keep it from your pa until I figure out a way to tell him. He'll think you're trying to get out of your chores."

"I'm *not* trying to get out of chores. I don't know where I am. Or who I am supposed to be. Show me what to do and I'll do it, but I don't know … remember. Is he a hard man? He looks very angry."

Clara looked at Jennifer with sadness. "Life has made him hard. He's had a difficult life. He's a good man but has worked so hard and it seems to get him nowhere. He wanted a boy and got you. He loves you in his way, but you're not strong like a son would be. Try to do what he says and you'll be all right."

"I'll try but you have to show me. Please tell me who I am and where I am."

"Your name is Josephine McKinley. I call you Josie and Pa calls you Jo. You're in De Soto, Wisconsin." *Where have I heard that town before?*

"What year is it?"

"1902."

All color left Jennifer's face and she felt herself go weak. She reached for the table for support and willed herself not to pass out. *1902. How can that be?* Jennifer eased herself onto a chair. She closed her eyes and took deep breaths trying to calm herself. She had gone back in time fifty-six more years. Why was this happening to her?

Clara touched her shoulder.

"Josie, are you all right?"

"No. Yes. I will be. I just have to get used to this. Please be patient with me."

"I will, but your pa won't. He isn't a patient man."

They finished putting food away and headed outside. Jennifer was glad to be where she could feel the fresh air and a little breeze. The house was stifling.

Clara took Jennifer to the garden to begin her job of weeding. The closer they got, the worse it looked. Except for one end of the garden, the weeds were overtaking everything.

"You had a start on this," Clara said, "but didn't get very far. If only you could concentrate on the task and not daydream so much."

"I'll try harder. Remind me which are the plants."

"I'll just do a little around each, so you can tell the plants from the weeds. You have to get this done."

Clara knelt down in the garden and began pulling weeds. As she worked, she explained. "We need these to get us through until next year's harvest. Potatoes, onions, carrots, beets. These are all root crops. These tall green stems are attached to the onion. Be careful when you pull weeds, so you don't pull the vegetables. These tall feather-like leaves are carrot tops. See the orange carrots poking through? The more room they have, the bigger they get. If they're too close together, they won't get very big. Thin the carrots and the onions as you go."

"What do you mean thin?" Jennifer asked.

"See, some carrots are too close to one another. After you weed them, pull the one in between. That will make room for the others to grow larger, wider." Clara showed Jennifer what she meant.

"You just throw them away then? With the weeds?"

"Oh, no! We eat them. Keep them separate."

"What about these? What are they?"

"Those are beets. If you get this far, you can thin those too. Keep the whole plant and I can make beet greens for supper. You know how Pa loves beet greens."

"OK."

Clara continued, "These are potatoes. They grow underneath on the roots. We dig them in the fall. After you get done weeding, you can water."

"How do I do that?"

"There's a stream just over yonder, down that little hill. It'll take some effort, but if you get this all done, Pa surely will be proud of you."

"I'll just sit and weed a little first. I'm still dizzy and my head hurts. When I feel stronger, I'll water some. Are there pails or what?"

"There are buckets, just inside the barn door."

Clara went back to the house and Jennifer started weeding onions. She didn't bother asking if they had a hoe because she had to get closer to the plants to see where they were. She didn't feel so lightheaded when she was sitting. The dry ground made pulling weeds hard but she kept at it, even though her hands were sore. *This is going to take a long time.*

Jennifer wiped sweat from her brow and looked across the land. *This would be very pretty if it wasn't so dry.* About thirty feet away, she could see a line of trees and the sparkling stream winding its course downstream.

As she worked, she thought about her problem. Why was this happening to her? How could she have been pulled back in time? Twice! She thought she was finally going home. Why had she been sent further back in time? She had no answers. And no idea how to get back home.

Yet as Jennifer weeded, she felt a deep satisfaction. It felt good to accomplish something.

Suddenly a shadow fell across her line of vision. Jennifer looked up to see Clyde standing over her. Jennifer scooted away. What had she done wrong now?

"Thought you might could use a drink," said Clyde. "You've been working steady. Maybe that hit on the head did you some good."

Tentatively, Jennifer reached for the cup and drank. She was amazed this angry man would think to bring her a drink of water. Cool and wet, just what she needed.

"Thank you," said Jennifer. "That was kind of you."

Clyde went back to work and so did Jennifer.

I guess I'll try to water some. She found two buckets in the barn and headed toward the stream. The ground was uneven and she had to be careful where she stepped. It would be easier, too, if she weren't wearing this dress that kept wrapping around her legs. When she reached the stream, she splashed cool water on her neck, face, and arms. She filled the buckets and started back to the garden, soon realizing how heavy they were. Her arms and shoulders ached from the strain and her hands hurt from the handles. She put the buckets down. Flexing her hands and rolling her shoulders, she relieved some of the discomfort. Gathering some of her dress to cushion her hands, she once again picked them up and headed toward the garden. *I bet I look like a dork trying to walk.*

Jennifer made it back to the garden and dropped the buckets. She wiped the sweat that dripped into her eyes with her dress. Her hands burned and her arms and shoulders screamed from the weight. She once again flexed her hands and rotated her shoulders to relieve the pain. Picking up one of the buckets, she began to water the garden.

It didn't take long to empty the buckets so she made another trip to the stream. She didn't fill them as full on the second trip but still struggled with the weight. Her hands and aching shoulders complained the whole way. Hard as it was, she made herself take another step, and another, and another. Tripping, she almost fell, spilling water. She stopped again to rest her sore muscles and hands, sweat pouring into her eyes and soaking her body. Picking the buckets up again, she started out, staggering over the rough ground. She tripped again, lost both of them and fell face first in the dirt.

She lay in the dirt, muddy from the spilled water. Exhaustion and frustration overwhelmed her and she began to cry. Pounding the dirt with her fist, she sobbed harder. *Why, God? Why am I here? Please help me!*

Jennifer heard running feet and looked up. Clyde was running toward her, his face frozen. Now she was in for it.

12

Missing Home

Clyde asked, "Are you all right?"

"Yes. I was just so hot and tired, and then I tripped and spilled the water. I'm sorry."

"Go clean up and head to the house. Rain's comin' anyway. No need to water."

"How do you know it's going to rain?" asked Jennifer, searching the empty sky.

"There's clouds forming on the horizon. See?" he said, pointing. "And I can feel it."

Jennifer looked where he pointed and saw a couple of small, white clouds far in the distance. She had her doubts about rain.

"Git now and clean up."

"I'll try and weed some more. No sense cleaning up before I finish. But I can't do those buckets of water."

A bewildered expression crossed Clyde's face but he said nothing further. He went back to hoeing the tobacco he had worked on all afternoon. If he could hoe in this heat, she could sit and weed a little more. *What if I end up staying here? I don't want to make him any madder than I already have.* It sounded like Josie should have finished the garden

70

by now. Maybe if Jennifer could get it done, it would help. A lot more work than she thought a garden would be. She continued with her task.

A short time later, Clara came out of the house.

"My land, Josie. You're almost done. I knew you could do it if you put your mind to it. Will you please take this to your pa? He could use a drink and this lard sandwich. When you get back, I have a sandwich for you waiting in the house, along with a drink."

Lard sandwich? I don't think so. "Um, I'm not really hungry."

Not happy to come in contact with Clyde again, Jennifer slowly headed toward the field. Clyde looked up, watching her approach.

"I brought you a sandwich and water. Clara sent it."

"Don't be callin' your ma Clara! You best respect her."

I can't believe it! He's talking to me about respect?

Jennifer yelled back. "You don't respect her! You treat her mean! You treat me mean! You treat everyone mean!" *So much for not making him mad.*

Jennifer turned quickly, trying to hide her tears. She didn't know if she could call them Ma and Pa. She had a mom, a dad, and a brother. She would sure give her mom more respect if—when—she got home again. *How could I ever think Mom was mean?*

Suddenly, she felt a great yearning to see her family again. She missed them terribly. She had enjoyed Harriet and Norman's farm, an experience she would treasure. They had been kind and Grace had become a fast friend.

But life was a lot harder here. She still couldn't understand *how* she got here. Or *why*. Would she have to spend the rest of her existence bouncing from one time period to another? She didn't want that! She wanted her own life back. She wanted her own mom, her own dad, and her own brother. She wanted her own house, her own friends, even the chance to clean her own room. She most of all wanted to tell her mom she was sorry and she loved her.

When Jennifer reached the garden, she sat down and cried. So lonely for her family, she could not control her tears. She hugged her knees, rocking back and forth, remembering when she was younger and her mom held her and rocked her whenever she was hurt or sad.

Please God. Please let me see my family again.

After a time, her tears spent, she wiped her eyes and nose with the hem of her dress. She couldn't just sit here and cry. That would do no good at all.

She had to figure out a way to blend into this life. Maybe telling Clara and Clyde the truth would work this time. No. She was pretty sure they wouldn't believe her any more than Harriet and Norman had. Should she just go ahead and tell Clyde she couldn't remember how to do stuff? Maybe that was still the best, so he wouldn't get mad when she didn't know how to do anything. Or would he think she was trying to get out of her chores?

Finishing the garden, she rinsed off in the stream. Perspiration soaked her dress. Her bonnet askew, her braids coming lose and hair hanging in damp curls, she walked slowly to the house. Bone tired, she made a decision.

"I should tell Clyde I don't remember anything," said Jennifer to Clara, as she walked into the house.

"Maybe I can help 'til you recollect."

"He can see how hard I worked all afternoon. He can see it's not to get out of work. Everything is so different ... I just don't know how ..."

"We'll see. I don't know. Let me think on it."

Clyde came in for supper and they sat down to eat. Clara had made a roast, added potatoes from last year's garden and the carrots and onions Jennifer thinned earlier. They had home-made bread. And beet greens which tasted bitter. She could not believe how much Clara and Clyde ate, both being so thin. They each ate enough for two people. *It must be all the hard work that keeps them thin.* She had been plenty hungry herself

72

after all her work.

Jennifer waited for Clara to tell Clyde about her amnesia. When she didn't, Jennifer spoke up.

"I can't remember," she said to Clyde.

"Can't remember what?" asked Clyde, taking a bite.

"I can't remember anything. I guess when I got run down by the wagon, I hit my head. I don't know who I am ... or how to do stuff ..."

"If this is your way of getting out of your chores, it won't work," Clyde said.

"No. You saw how hard I worked today. I finished the garden and tried to water. It's not to get out of work. I'll do the chores. You just have to tell me what to do and show me how to do it."

"I seen you in the garden and you done a good job. Maybe like I said, it knocked some sense into you. After dishes, milk the cows. That's your next chore."

Jennifer breathed a sigh of relief. That wasn't so bad. Now she didn't have to pretend to remember something she never knew.

Clara heated the water for dishes. She washed while Jennifer dried. Jennifer started singing like she and Harriet had done.

"What is that song?" asked Clara. "It sounds familiar."

"It's 'Amazing Grace.' Singing is fun and helps the time go faster."

"It's curious you forget some things but remember songs," Clara said.

Saying nothing further, Clara joined Jennifer and when they finished singing "Amazing Grace," they sang "Jesus Loves Me" and "What A Friend We Have in Jesus."

"I recollect Mama singing those when I was a child. It's been many years since I heard those songs," Clara said.

"Don't you ... we go to church?"

"The preacher comes around once a month, but your pa has no time for church."

After finishing dishes, Jennifer headed out to milk the cows. Clara went with her and showed her where the stool and pails were. Jennifer was thankful for her short lesson on the farm. *Thank God there are only three cows.* She sat down to milk her first cow, trying to remember everything Norman had shown her. She washed their teats before she started and began milking.

"You sure are taking your time with the cows tonight," Clyde said, entering the barn.

Give me a break! "I need to remember how and my hands are sore from weeding. I'll get it."

When finished milking, she let the cows back out in the pasture. Clyde hauled the milk pails away but Jennifer hadn't noticed a milk house. Maybe it was that little shed she had seen earlier.

Jennifer walked into the kitchen and asked, "What happens to the milk?"

"It's in the cellar where we usually keep it," replied Clara.

"Can I see? How is it kept cool?"

"Just go around the back and lift the cellar doors. As soon as you go down, you'll recollect the cellar. Don't dally and let in a lot of hot air."

Jennifer walked around the house to the cellar doors. Two doors, each about three feet by five, lay almost flat with the ground. Meeting in the middle, each had a handle for lifting. She grabbed one to lift. It was heavy. Using all her strength, she managed to open one side and walked down the steps, amazed at the difference in temperature.

Finding a small, chest-like cabinet, she opened its door and saw the milk, a small amount of butter, and some meat. In a drawer above the door she saw a chunk of ice almost melted. This would keep things cool for a while, but where did they get the ice?

Ascending the steps, she felt the rise in temperature. She remembered to close the cellar door tightly and went back to the kitchen.

"Where does the ice come from? In this heat, it sure won't last long."

Clara answered with wearied patience, "We get it from the ice shed like always. We cut it in winter from the stream and pack it for use as long as it lasts."

"Pack it in what? What keeps ice this long when its this warm?"

"We pack it in sawdust and straw. You act like you never heard such a thing."

"I'm sorry. I really don't know."

"Your pa is about ready to haul a chunk of ice to the cellar. If you go quick, you can see where he gets it."

Jennifer found Clyde outside with large tongs. Going into the little shed she saw earlier, he moved some straw and reached down into the pile with the tongs, lifting a piece of ice to put in the cooler.

Jennifer went back to the house and asked Clara, "What happens if you run out of ice? How do you keep things cool?"

"Late in the summer, we oftentimes use the well."

"You mean, you put things in the water?"

"Some things, like milk, we hang on a rope and let down just above the water."

***

Evening came, the three of them sitting on the porch resting from their long day. The breeze, cooler now, was a welcome contrast to the heat of the day. Gusts of wind swirled leaves and dust across the lawn. Gray storm clouds loomed in the west, thunder rumbling in the distance.

"Sounds like it's going to rain, like you said," said Jennifer, trying to make conversation.

"Yep. Like I said. I could feel it," replied Clyde.

"The breeze sure feels good," said Clara. "It will be good to get rain."

When Clara and Clyde went to bed, Jennifer sat alone on the porch. She thought about the differences here, way harder than her life at home. This was a small shack with basic living quarters, food, necessities. No frills. No television. No radio. No computers or phones. Not even a pump. Mom and Dad worked hard too, but modern conveniences sure made life easier.

But here, she also hadn't noticed any fun or joy or laughter. Only hard work. Not like at home where they didn't work *all* the time. She spent a lot of time with her friends and family. Together, they could enjoy almost anything. But here, there didn't appear to be anything joyful. *Please God. Help me get back.*

Later that night, she sneaked around the back of the house with a bar of soap. Standing in the rain in her underwear, she breathed in the freshness. It felt like an eternity since she had had a real shower, her parched skin soaking up the coolness of the summer rain. She soaped her hair and then her face, neck, arms, legs and feet. The soap had a strange smell, not the peach scent of the shower gel she liked to use at home. She didn't care. This was the cleanest she felt since this whole nightmare adventure started.

Jennifer jumped at Clara's voice. "What are you doing out in this rain?"

I thought she was asleep. Jennifer grabbed her clothes and covered herself.

"I'm taking a shower. The rain feels wonderful and I needed to get the dirt and sweat off."

"This is more than a shower. This is a storm and there's lightning on the horizon. You best get inside."

Quickly, Jennifer dressed and headed inside where Clyde sat in his nightshirt.

"Just when I thought you got some sense in you," said Clyde, "you go and stand out in the storm. You *must* be addle-brained. Go on up to bed now," he said, nodding at the ladder. "Git some rest."

Jennifer slowly climbed the ladder leading up to the loft. She saw a small sleeping area made up on the floor, the mattress homemade with what felt like straw for padding. In the small, brown dresser she found a nightgown. Donning it quickly, she felt almost human again. Stuffy and hot in the loft, she didn't know if she could sleep.

Jennifer listened to the rain on the roof for a long time. Rain had always been soothing to her and she felt calmer now. She had worked hard, eaten well, had a shower, and her headache was gone! *Thank you, God.*

Sometimes at home when it was storming, the power would go out. Mom and Dad would set out candles and they played fun games so Ryan wouldn't get scared. But it was always an adventure for her.

The rain turned into a full-blown storm, lightning flashing across the sky followed by big cracks of thunder. At some point, it turned back to a nice summer rain and lulled her to sleep.

She awoke in the morning, surprised she had slept so well. She rolled out of bed, wondering what the day would bring.

13

Chores

Breakfast consisted of eggs, bacon, fresh bread, and homemade raspberry jam. Jennifer asked the question she had been dreading, "What chores do I have today?"

"We need to churn butter and wash clothes," said Clara. "You can pick which you'd prefer."

Jennifer had no idea what churning butter consisted of and said, "I guess I could wash clothes. I think I remember liking that."

Again, Jennifer got the "you're crazy" look, this time from Clara. Right now, Jennifer's whole life was crazy.

After doing breakfast dishes, Clara began preparations for washing clothes. She went to the stove, which had four burners, an oven, and a rectangular section Jennifer was unfamiliar with. Clara stuck a cast iron handle into a groove in the rectangular section, lifting the lid and poured water into what turned out to be a boiler. Replacing the lid, she then took the edge of her apron, using it as an oven mitt, opened another section of the stove, threw in a couple pieces of wood, and closed it again. No wonder the house was so warm. They had a wood stove going when it was already hot outside! Why had she not realized this was the only source for heating and cooking. What about electricity?

How can I wash clothes without electricity?

Going outside, Clara set up two round, gray, galvanized metal washtubs under the only tree in the front yard. Each tub was about two feet in diameter and ten inches deep. From a hook on the porch, she grabbed a washboard which had a wooden frame, fifteen inches long by seven inches wide, with a piece of corrugated metal attached in the middle. She grabbed a bar of soap from a kitchen shelf and headed back outside. *This is nothing like doing clothes on the farm.*

"I don't know how to do this," said Jennifer.

"You mean you don't recollect. Would you rather churn butter?"

"I don't know how ... remember that either. Just show me."

Going to the well, Clara turned the handle to which a rope and bucket were attached, dropping it until she heard a splash. She dipped it until it was filled with water and then cranked the handle again, bringing the bucket back to the top. Clara poured the water into another pail.

"You can go dump this into one of the tubs for rinsing," Clara told Jennifer.

As requested, Jennifer dumped the water and made two more trips to fill the tub. Going back into the house, Jennifer watched as Clara took a large dipper and transferred hot water from the boiler into a pail and carried it to the second wash tub, which already had some well water. With a knife, she then grated a little soap from a bar into the water, and showed Jennifer how to wash clothes on a washboard.

"Start with the light clothes," Clara said. "Get them wet and then rub up and down on the washboard, moving it around to all spots to get clean. If there's an especially soiled spot, rub more soap from the bar onto that section and rub up and down again on the washboard." Clara took a dish towel showing Jennifer how to do it. "Then put it in the rinse tub. You can do several pieces at a time. After rinsing a few, wring them out and hang them on the line to dry."

Jennifer reached for a light-colored apron and went to work. She pushed the apron into the water. Yelping in pain, she jerked her hands back out. The hot water hurt her hands, still sore from weeding. Steeling herself, she went back to work. Gently, she took the apron and rubbed it up and down on the washboard as Clara had instructed. Up and down. Up and down. After washing each piece, she put it in the rinse tub. After only a few items, her arms already ached. Now, her knuckles were sore and raw. *If I ever do get home, I'll be one big, sore mess.*

"I'm ready to hang some. Where is the line?"

"Right around the corner of the house," Clara pointed.

Jennifer swished the water to rinse the items thoroughly. Taking one piece at a time, she squeezed the water from each item and dropped it in a basket, until her rinse tub was empty. Going to the clothesline, she again wrung every piece to remove more water, and hung it up to dry.

Jennifer scanned the countryside. The rain had made a wonderful difference, greening up the landscape. Singing bluebirds flew overhead, brown robins hopped along the ground pecking for worms, and a couple of gray squirrels chased each other around a tree. Yellow, white, and lilac wild flowers blanketed the field behind the house. She would love to sit down and enjoy the landscape. *Too much work to do to be woolgathering,* she heard Clyde in her head.

It took Jennifer all morning to do a few clothes; four dresses, two aprons, a pair of overalls, two shirts, socks, underwear, and a dish cloth and towel. Her knuckles were bleeding and her arms ached. It's a good thing people didn't have a lot of clothes back in the old days. Nothing relaxing about washing clothes. Just hard work.

While Jennifer was doing laundry, Clara set up a butter churn by a stool on the porch. It looked like a wooden barrel, the top smaller than the bottom, with a wooden handle sticking out of the top. Clara skimmed the cream from the milk and poured it into the churn. She sat on a stool and began moving the handle up and down, up and down.

"Come butter come. Come butter come. Peter stands at the gate

80

waiting for the buttered cake," Clara sang as she worked.

"What is that song?"

"An old rhyme I learned years ago from my mama. It takes so long to get butter it helps the time go faster."

"That looks a lot easier than this. I guess I should have chosen that job."

"It's all hard work. This is just the beginning. After I do this for maybe an hour, the butter begins to form. I'll then need to rinse and drain several times. Then I add the salt and press out the extra moisture."

Jennifer thought it still looked easier than washing clothes on a washboard. If only she had known.

"Tell me about our life ... so I can remember," said Jennifer. "How long have you lived here?"

"Oh, my, we've lived here in this homestead maybe fifteen years. Yes. It was 1887, the year I turned 16. It seems like forever. You were born here."

"In this house? Wow! Did you have ... do I have brothers or sisters?"

"We had a baby boy who died. Joseph. That's his grave over there," Clara said pointing. "I couldn't have any more."

Jennifer looked where Clara pointed and saw a small white cross.

"I'm sorry. Is that why Clyde is so angry?"

"Some."

"What happened to his leg?"

"When he was a boy, he had a farm accident. He injured his leg trying to do something he was too young for."

"Why did they let him?"

"He was so proud of his daddy and wanted to help, would do anything for him. Like others, he came home injured from the war ..."

"What war?"

"The War to Preserve the Union. Some call it the Civil War but there was nothing civil about it. He came home and was able to carry on but it was hard. Clyde had two older brothers who helped and as soon as Clyde was old enough, he helped all he could. They thought he would lose his leg, but they saved it. He still has pain, but he's determined to keep going."

Jennifer's perception of Clyde changed. Clyde had a hard life. His father was injured in the Civil War. Clyde almost lost a leg himself, and then lost a son. From that moment, Jennifer was determined to help Clyde in any way she could. She didn't know how. *But I can do something to help alleviate his suffering, something to make a difference in his life.*

14

Prejudice

J ennifer finished the last of the wash and emptied the tubs, thinking about what Clara had told her. She thought how easy it is for people to make quick judgments about others. Once she heard a little about Clyde's background, she understood why he was so angry. His life had been hard and he worked every day with pain. He didn't complain and he didn't make excuses. He did what had to be done to feed his family. Still, no reason to be so mean to Clara or Josie. No reason to be mean to anyone.

"Josie, let's get some lunch on. Pa will be in soon."

While they ate, Jennifer asked Clyde, "Is there something I can do to help after lunch?"

Taken aback, brow furrowed, he answered, "If your ma don't need you, I have fences to mend. You could help with that if you've a mind to."

Jennifer looked at Clara who nodded her approval.

"I could do that ... if you show me how."

After lunch, Jennifer and Clyde started out together. Clyde grabbed a roll of barbed wire and some posts. Jennifer carried water for drinking and an odd-looking shovel.

"Here, put these on," said Clyde, giving her a pair of gloves.

"Thank you. What can I do to help?"

"I need to dig some holes for posts to strengthen the fence line. You can help me secure the posts when I get that far."

The post hole digger had a double blade, like two metal shovels facing each other, but not as large. Each shovel had a handle five feet long that opened up like tongs. Jennifer watched as Clyde took the digger, opened the handles so the shovel blades were about eight inches apart, and drove it into the ground. Pulling the handles farther apart and the shovels together, Clyde brought up six inches of dirt in one grab. Repeating this maneuver several times, Clyde had a hole deep enough to drop a post into. Jennifer helped pack dirt to keep it standing firm and helped Clyde wrap barbed-wire around the post. She then unraveled enough wire to wrap around the next one as they moved on to dig another hole.

Jennifer wanted to say something to Clyde about what she had learned from Clara. She wanted to tell him she thought he was brave, to somehow make it better for him—if she could.

Clyde interrupted her thoughts. "You're not the same."

Alarmed, Jennifer said, "What? How?"

"Seems to me after you was hit by the runaway wagon, you're different. You sure worked hard this afternoon, not woolgathering as usual. Telling me I was rude and mean. Can't say as I liked hearing that much."

"I'm sorry."

"No. You were right. My pappy was hurt and had a hard life. But he never was mean to my mamma, nor none of us. He took in strangers when he could. I wasn't raised to be mean."

Getting up her nerve, Jennifer said, "Clara ... Ma told me a little about your life, about losing a son and your daddy being in the Civil War. I think he was brave and I think you're brave, after all you've been through in your life."

"I did what I had to. Twernt no more than anyone else."

"Yes. Some people would just give up. You didn't. You kept going."

"I had to. I have a family to care for. My pa fought in the Civil War for what he believed, for what was right. He came back wounded and kept going for his family and so do I. I just wish *his* suffering would have meant more."

"What do you mean?"

"He fought for the Negro. For their right to have their own life. To be free. I don't see that things have changed much since then."

Jennifer thought about what Clyde said. He seemed more upset by his daddy's pain than what he was going through himself. He wanted his daddy's suffering to be worth something, for the war to have helped the Negro. Jennifer had studied the Civil War in school. Could she tell Clyde she *knew* it made a difference?

Clyde continued, "We have a memorial service every year—a parade and a few speeches. For those who fought in the war, for some who didn't come back, and a few who did. But I don't see where it made a lot of difference. I still hear and see how people treat the Negro. There's a lot of prejudice yet."

"It will get better," said Jennifer. "I know it will."

"How can you know that? You can't just daydream things into being."

No, you couldn't daydream things into being. You had to make them happen. If she told Clyde what she *knew* to be the future, would he believe her? Maybe that's why she was sent here, to tell Clyde his daddy's sacrifice *did* make a difference.

Saying a quick prayer, Jennifer continued, "I know this will be hard to believe, but please listen to me. I'm not Josie … Jo. I'm Jennifer. I was transported here the day of the runaway wagon. That's why I can't remember. I don't belong here. That's why I'm different."

"Don't start that. You're making things up again."

"I know it seems impossible but I'm living it. *Please* believe me. I *know* that things will get better for the Negro."

"How can you know? How can I believe such a crazy thing?" Jennifer could tell from Clyde's voice he *wanted* to. He *needed* to know his daddy had not fought in vain.

"I came from the year 2009. I don't know how. I only know it happened and I don't know how to get home. But I do know that life is better for many black people. We have black mayors, congressman, doctors, lawyers. Just like anybody else, a black person can be anything he or she wants to be if they work for it. We even have a black president now, the first one ever. His name is Barack Obama."

Clyde's face went through a kaleidoscope of expressions: disbelief, incredulity, uncertainty, hope, back to disbelief.

"How could you come from another time? It don't make sense. It ain't possible."

"I don't know how, but I'm not making it up." Jennifer dropped the matter. At least Clyde hadn't called her a liar outright.

They worked steadily for another hour, Clyde giving her sideways looks. Jennifer wondered if he was weighing what she had told him. Of all the people she had met on her adventure, she didn't think Clyde would be one to believe her. Maybe he did.

This is taking a long time and I'm already tired.

Speaking her thoughts out loud, she said, "This is hard work. Maybe you need a man around to help you keep up. Someone stronger. You could *hire* a black man. Some guy who needs a job."

"I can't pay no extra help. I barely manage to keep this place going."

"Maybe someone would work for food and a place to sleep."

"I'll think on it. Let's head back to the house. Your ma … Clara … will have supper ready soon."

Jennifer recognized Clyde's indecision and felt a small triumph. *Maybe he's trying to believe me.*

After supper, Clyde headed back out to finish the fence line, while

Jennifer stayed to help with dishes. Soon after starting, they heard Clyde yell.

"Clara! Jo! Come quick! The cows are out!"

Clara and Jennifer ran.

"They're right there," said Clyde, pointing. "They got a whiff of that clover and took off. Jo, you try and get in front of the cows and head them toward the barn. Ma and I'll take each side and try to keep them going in the right direction."

Jennifer didn't want to chase a cow. She wasn't afraid of them when they were in the barn but what if they charged her? She didn't think she could stand up to a cow. She headed across the field where Clyde directed her, not at all sure what to do.

Slowly, they worked their way around the cows so as not to spook them where they were eating in a nice green spot. All three managed to persuade the cows to move toward the barn. As they reached the barnyard, one cow tried to get past Jennifer and she moved quickly to cut her off. She headed it back in the right direction, but in her effort, slipped on a cow pie and fell. Sitting in the oozing manure, she tried to get up without making it worse. She reached down to push herself up and put her hand into the squishy, still warm, ooze. By the time she got to her feet, it had soaked through her clothes. Her right hand was full of the disgusting mess. She discovered in a short time that "fresh" cow pie does not smell good. She reeked. She looked up at Clara and Clyde. As they came toward her, she thought she saw them smile. By the time they reached her, they were both laughing.

"You think this is pretty hilarious, don't you?" asked Jennifer.

Laughing too hard to speak, Clara and Clyde could only nod. Surprised, Jennifer said, "I'm glad you think this is so funny. It's worth it to see you enjoying yourselves."

When they had controlled themselves, Clara said, "You need to get some of that off before you come in the house. Wash up at the creek first. Take your dress off and rinse it good."

Jennifer headed for the creek, holding her right hand away from her. On the way, she thought about her brother, Ryan. He would get a kick out of chasing cows. He would feel like a cowboy. And to see her fall in the mess! He would tell the world about that. She wished she could give him a hug right now, manure and all.

Jennifer reached the creek and went right in, dress and all. She swished her hand in the water. When the ripples began to subside, she noticed something in the water. Almost reaching for it, she pulled back. The hair on the back of her neck stood up. Shivers ran down her spine. Was this going to be another "time warp?" If so, would she be going home? Or would she be sent back another fifty years? Or a hundred?

While getting up her courage and waiting for the ripples to clear, she saw her. It looked like Josie. It could be Julie. She couldn't tell. They looked so much alike.

This was it then. Another "time warp." She decided to take her chances. She couldn't get home by staying here. Saying a quick prayer, she reached into the water.

Immediately, she felt the familiar pull.

15

Home Again

Once again spinning out of control, Jennifer wondered where she would land next. Why did this keep happening? Was she finally going home? She missed Mom, Dad, and Ryan. She missed Paige and she missed Kelly. She missed her shower and her music and her computer. She missed *everything*. To avoid feeling sick, she again kept her eyes closed. It was taking even longer than the second time to "fall out." Did that mean she was going back further?

Afraid of the extended time, she gritted her teeth against the nausea and opened her eyes. Not completely black as before, she saw things swirling around her. Flashes of color. Flashes of light. Other girls. Different clothes. Different hair. Did one have a long dress and bonnet? Could it be Josie? The spinning made it hard to focus. Were there two girls? Or four? Could they see her? Someone was screaming. Why could she see them now and not the first two times? Was someone waving at her?

Feeling sick to her stomach, Jennifer closed her eyes again. Suddenly, she was no longer spinning but falling. She tried not to scream. Coming to an abrupt stop, she hit hard.

She heard running feet.

"Jen, are you all right?"

Her eyes popped open. It was Mom! Mom! Lying at the bottom of the stairs, Jennifer began to cry. Bawling, she couldn't talk.

"Are you hurt? Did you fall down the stairs again?" asked Mom.

Jennifer tried to stop her tears. She had no idea if she'd fallen down the stairs. It felt like it, but she knew she was all right.

"I'm home. I'm really home. Thank you, God. I'm so sorry, Mom," Jennifer said between sobs.

"Of course, you're home. Where did you think you were?"

Taking deep breaths, Jennifer tried to control herself. She wanted to explain and she *needed* Mom to believe her.

"I'm OK, but I have to tell you where I've been. What day is it?"

Concern in her eyes, Mom said, "It's Wednesday."

"Wednesday! I left Saturday! I've been gone for five days?"

"Jen, you're scaring me."

"I'm OK, Mom. I promise. Please listen."

"If you're sure. But, let's get you off the floor."

Mom helped Jennifer up and they went into the living room and sat down.

"OK, I'm listening."

"I know this is going to sound crazy. I can hardly believe it myself. Please, listen and know I *am not* making it up." *How many times have I said that?* Jennifer continued, "Remember when we had that fight on Saturday, when you wouldn't let me go to Take Five? By the way, I'm sorry I called you mean. I was just mad. I love you, Mom."

"I remember and you're forgiven."

"I was so upset and then, when I went into the bathroom to wash my face, I just ... sort of ... was pulled into the mirror." Rushing on before her mom could call her nuts, she said, "I was at a farm somewhere in Wisconsin in 1958. Then, I was pulled into the wash water and landed somewhere different, in 1902. I know it sounds unbelievable but it really happened! I was afraid I would never get back home and here I am! I'm so glad!" Jennifer started crying again and Mom wrapped her arms around her.

After a while, Mom said, "I won't say I don't believe you. I can see you really believe this happened. Some dreams are so real. It must have been a dream."

"It wasn't a dream. I know it wasn't. I'm just so glad to be home again."

Ryan skipped into the room and Jennifer gave a yelp of glee. She ran over and gave him a big hug.

"Ryan, it's so good to see you. I missed you so much."

"I was just over by Timmy for a while."

Jennifer laughed, delighted to be home.

Mom said, "When Dad gets home, we'll tell him your story and see what he thinks.

Later, after hearing Jennifer's story, Dad stared at her in disbelief.

"Jennifer, I know you've never been one to make things up, but this is incredible. How can we believe this really happened? It must have been a dream like Mom said."

"I don't know how to convince you it wasn't a dream. If it was, it sure seemed real. I got to milk cows and feed calves. Both places had big gardens. One was well kept and the other needed lots of work. Josie was supposed to do that, but she didn't. I would love to have a vegetable garden someday. Do you think maybe we could start one next spring?"

Dad said, "We'll see. If you show you can stick to it, maybe we'll put in a few things. Your mom and I don't have time for that, so you would have to do most of the work."

"That would be great! Maybe we could go fishing too. I got to go fishing and it wasn't at all boring, like I thought. It was fun. That's the day I met Grace and she's awesome."

Surprised, Dad said, "I would like that a lot."

"I got to wash clothes in an old-fashioned washing machine and hang them on the line. I really enjoyed that, but not the washboard. Oh! My hands are blistered and bleeding from the washboard." Jennifer looked at her hands. No blistering. No bleeding.

"I don't understand it. Just today, I was washing clothes outside with a washboard. It was really hard work. My hands were bleeding and hurt a lot."

Mom and Dad looked at her with an "I told you so" expression but didn't say anything. Jennifer was so confused. She *knew* she had experienced all of this. Not a dream, but real life, a real fantastic life.

"I picked up a pizza on the way home from work," Dad said. "Let's eat."

"I want to say grace," Jennifer announced, as they sat down.

Mom and Dad looked at one another, eyes wide and eyebrows raised.

"This is a day of surprises," Mom said. "Maybe something did happen to you."

Something did happen to me. Something I'll never forget!

Jennifer bowed her head, saying, "Thank you, God, for all You've shown me, for keeping me safe. Thank You for this food and especially for bringing me back home. Amen."

"That was nice, Jen. Thank you," said Mom.

Jennifer said, "This is so good. I bet Julie and Josie never got pizza. I didn't see any fast food places. They sure ate good on the farms though. Not one of them was fat. It must be all the hard work."

When finished eating, Jennifer said, "I'll wash the dishes, Mom. Maybe Ryan could dry. It's always more fun with two."

"That sounds like a good idea. Would you like that, Ryan?" Mom asked.

"Do I have to?" Ryan whined.

"It won't hurt you," Mom said.

Jennifer cleared the table with Ryan's help. Jennifer filled the sink, marveling at the hot running water. Why had she acted like such a baby and complained about *everything?*

While Ryan and Jennifer did dishes, they sang a few songs to make the time go faster. Ryan knew "Twinkle Twinkle Little Star" and "Jesus Loves Me" and Jennifer taught him some of "Amazing Grace." It would always be her favorite.

"I guess you feel happy today. You sure were sad before," Ryan said.

"Why? When was I sad?"

"I don't know. You were crying and said you wanted to go home. You were acting funny, like you didn't remember anything."

"Like what?"

"You didn't know how to use the microwave to cook mac and cheese for me. Or how to use the remote for the TV. You sat in front of the computer like you didn't even know what it was. You hated the noise outside. You said you could *never* get used to that."

Julie or Josie must have been here while I was gone.

***

A month later when Jennifer and Ryan were finishing dishes, she heard the doorbell. Giving Ryan a kiss on the cheek, Jennifer said, "Thanks Ryan. You're a good helper."

Mom poked her head in the kitchen and said, "Jen, two ladies are here to see you."

"Who are they?"

"I don't know. I've never seen them."

Jennifer followed Mom to the door.

"These women say they know you," said Mom.

Jennifer looked at them and tried to remember who they were. They were both really old.

"I'm sorry. Where have we met?"

"I'm Grace. I believe we met about fifty years ago, and this is Julie."

"Oh my gosh!" said Jennifer. "Is it really you, Grace? And Julie!"

Grace laughed and said, "We've been waiting all this time to come and visit you. It was over fifty years ago, you know, for us. We brought the note you wrote when you were on the farm so we had your name and address. We just had to wait until we thought you were back from the adventure."

"I can't believe you're here! I just saw you and you were my age!" said Jennifer.

"I can't believe this really happened," said Mom. "We thought it must have been a dream."

"Come in," said Jennifer. To Julie, she said, "You have to tell me where you were when I was on your farm."

"I was here part of the time. Hi, Ryan. Do you remember me?"

"No," Ryan said, hiding behind his mom. "Who are you?"

"My name is Julie and I was here when Jennifer was gone. Remember when you helped me with the microwave? You made me macaroni and cheese because I didn't know how to do it."

"No, that was Jennifer. She just forgot."

Jennifer said, "Remember, Ryan, when I was saying I was at a farm a long time ago?"

"I guess," Ryan said.

"Well, when I was gone, Julie was here instead of me. That's when you said I was sad and didn't know anything."

Ryan's eyes widened and he looked from Jennifer to Julie and back again.

"But you don't look like Jennifer. You're old."

Laughing, Jennifer thought she'd better give it up. He would understand the time difference someday.

As they seated themselves in the living room, Jennifer said to Julie, "When Ryan told me I was sad and didn't know anything, I wondered if maybe you had been here, or Josie."

"Josie? Do you mean Josie McKinley?"

"Yes. I was in her life, in 1902. That was a *real* adventure. I really liked

94

your farm, but in Josie's time, it was such hard work to do anything. Do you know Josie?"

"Josie is a lady who lived in our area a long time ago. People said she was always dreaming of a faraway adventure in a different time. She spoke of being in a place with so many people. So many fancy machines and automobiles and noise. No one believed her, except her daddy. She finally quit talking about it. She became a school teacher and taught children to dream big because whatever they could think of, they could do."

"Her daddy believed her?" asked Jennifer.

"That's the story. They say he was the only one."

"Did you enjoy your adventures?" asked Grace.

"It seems like each time warp was really different. I used to complain all the time because I had chores to do and would rather do something else. Josie's life was hard, but it was simple. Because of that time, now I appreciate more what I have. Even simple things like rain, indoor plumbing, electricity. Even though I enjoyed your farm and everything about it, I really missed home. I missed my family and my friends and my own life. This is the life God gave me and I promise to always treasure every part of it."

About the Author

The inspiration for Mirror Image came from the author's time spent on her grandparents' farm as a child. Stories about time travel have always intrigued her. It seemed fitting to combine the two in her first chapter book for preteens.

The author, wife, mother of three and grandmother of four is a retired legal secretary, who now has time to pursue the writing she has loved all her life.

Born and raised in Wisconsin, she lives with her husband, Greg, and their black lab, Bear, in northern Wisconsin.

Made in the USA
Monee, IL
08 September 2022